# The Seven Wonders
# of Sassafras Springs

# The Seven Wonders
# of Sassafras Springs

BETTY G. BIRNEY
Illustrated by Matt Phelan

**Aladdin Paperbacks**
NEW YORK   LONDON   TORONTO   SYDNEY

This book is a work of fiction. Any references to historical events, real people, or real locales are used fictitiously. Other names, characters, places, and incidents are the product of the author's imagination, and any resemblance to actual events or locales or persons, living or dead, is entirely coincidental.

ALADDIN PAPERBACKS
An imprint of Simon & Schuster Children's Publishing Division
1230 Avenue of the Americas, New York, NY 10020
Text copyright © 2005 by Betty G. Birney
Illustrations copyright © 2005 by Matt Phelan
All rights reserved, including the right of reproduction in whole or in part in any form.
ALADDIN PAPERBACKS and colophon are trademarks of Simon & Schuster, Inc.
Also available in an Atheneum Books for Young Readers hardcover edition.
The text of this book was set in Lomba.
The illustrations for this book were rendered in pencil and ink.
Manufactured in the United States of America
First Aladdin Paperbacks edition February 2007
10  9  8  7  6  5  4  3
The Library of Congress has cataloged the hardcover edition as follows:
Birney, Betty G.
The seven wonders of Sassafras Springs / Betty G. Birney.—1st ed.
p.cm.
Summary: Eben McAllister searches his small town to see if he can find anything comparable to the real Seven Wonders of the World.
ISBN-13: 978-0-689-87136-8 (hc)
ISBN-10: 0-689-87136-8 (hc)
[1. Wonder—Fiction. 2. Country life—Fiction. 3. Family life—Fiction. 4. Neighbors—Fiction.] I. Title
PZ7.B52285Se 2005  [Fic]—dc22  2004011399
ISBN-13: 978-1-4169-3489-9 (pbk)
ISBN-10: 1-4169-3489-8 (pbk)

To the many wonderful storytellers in my family, especially my father, Ed Griesbaum, who has preserved the stories of two families and carved a magical village of his own.

To the memory of my grandmother, Ella Hinson Mohrmann, who enthralled and delighted my sister and me with her stories of growing up in the country.

To the memory of my mother, Ella Mohrmann Griesbaum, and my grandfather, Herman Mohrmann, who both loved to tell a good story.

To my editor, Caitlyn Dlouhy, the Eighth Wonder of Sassafras Springs!

And, finally, to good storytellers everywhere.

—B. G. B.

# Contents

How It Started    1

Day One: I Go Searching    13
Mrs. Pritchard's Story: Miss Zeldy's Message

Day Two: Jeb Joins In    35
Cully Pone's Story: The Rainmaker's Revenge

Day Three: Disappointments    63

Day Three Continued: Difficulties and Discoveries    73
Calvin Smiley's Story: Amazing Grace

Day Four: Smells and Spells    95
Eulie Rowan's Story: The Four-Legged Haint

Day Five: Into the Woods    117
Coogie Jackson's Story: Flight from Georgia
Rae Ellen's Story: Dark Seas

Days Six and Seven: I Start Again    153
Mayor Peevey's Story: Song of the Loom

Day Eight: A Setback and a Surprise    179
Uncle Alf's Story: Graven Images

Day Nine: Change of Plans    199

The Beginning    207

# The Seven Wonders
# of Sassafras Springs

# How It Started

Sometimes extraordinary things begin in ordinary places. A fancy-dancy butterfly starts out in a plain little cocoon. A great big apple tree grows from a tiny brown speck of a seed. And the Wonders started right on our own front porch on a hot summer night I would have forgotten on the spot if it hadn't been for what got started then and kept on going.

Who knows, maybe Columbus decided to look for a New World one hot summer night when he got tired of staring at the same old barn. Or maybe one evening after supper, Balboa stood up and said, "Excuse me now, folks. I'm going to search for the Pacific Ocean."

There was no chance of seeing an ocean in Sassafras Springs, which is set smack dab in the center of the country. Though a dip in Liberty Creek was welcome on a boiling hot day, to my mind it was a poor excuse for a body of water. Shoot, it wasn't even a dribble on the big map of the United States that hung on the schoolhouse wall.

Red Hawk, Coy, and Iron Valley all had dots on the map, but not Sassafras Springs, Missouri. We might as well have been invisible, yet there I was, sitting on the front porch with Pa and Aunt Pretty. The chores were done, our bellies were full, and the mosquitoes hadn't worked up much of an appetite yet.

Aunt Pretty sat in her high-back rocker, crocheting some lacy thing as usual, though for the life of me I couldn't make out what it was meant to be. I hoped it wasn't intended for me. Pa whittled on a stick and I was staring hard at a drawing in a book. It was a first-rate book with lots of pictures in it. Miss Collins, the schoolteacher, gave it to me on the last day of school for getting the best marks in geography.

My mind was a million miles away when suddenly my aunt said, "Eben McAllister, you've had your nose in that book so long, I forgot what you look like! Wake up and see the world."

I gazed out at the familiar white fence, the faded

red barn, and the yellow clay road. A pair of fireflies blinked over Aunt Pretty's peony bed. Our horses, Pat and Murph, were in the barn, Mabel and Myrt were milked, and the chickens had gone to bed long ago. My dog, Sal, thumped her tail, most likely hoping I would stir up some excitement. She should have known better.

"Nothing to see," I said and went back to my book. Sal rolled on her side and yawned.

"You'd think someone would have something interesting to say about *something*," Aunt Pretty said. "Living with the two of you is like living alone. I might as well talk to myself."

Although I didn't say it, Aunt Pretty did talk to herself, all day long. It was no picnic taking care of Pa and me. She moved in when Ma died four years ago and did all she could. Still, it was lonely for her because Aunt Pretty could talk your arm off, while Pa and I weren't ones to waste words.

"What's so interesting about that book, anyway?" Aunt Pretty asked.

"It's about the Seven Wonders of the World," I told her. "They built these amazing things way back in ancient Greece and Egypt and places."

Pa blew the shavings off his stick. "What things?" he asked.

I showed him the book, and he took his time studying the drawings. He read the names out loud, and they sounded fine. The Great Pyramid at Giza. The Colossus of Rhodes. The Statue of Zeus. The giant Lighthouse at Alexandria. The Mausoleum at Halicarnassus. The Temple of Artemis at Ephesus. The Hanging Gardens of Babylon. Big things. Wonderful things.

"We don't have anything like that around Sassafras Springs," I pointed out.

"We do have the wash hanging on the line every Monday," Aunt Pretty chuckled. "Call it the Hanging Laundry of Sassafras Springs and put it in a book. There's your Wonder."

I tried to make her understand. "These were *important* things. In faraway lands."

Aunt Pretty sniffed loudly. "Seems to me we have lighthouses right here in the U.S.A."

"Not like this one. This light could be seen for thirty miles. Fires burned behind the eyes. See?" I held up the page with a drawing of the Lighthouse at Alexandria, but my aunt barely glanced at it.

Pa calmly scraped away at his stick of wood. "I guess I could put some eyes up on the side of the barn, but I'm afraid the fires would scare the horses."

I didn't give him the satisfaction of a comeback.

"I suppose we all have notions that others might find peculiar," Aunt Pretty said.

"Everyone except you, Pretty." Pa's voice was teasinglike.

"You hush up, Cole, or I'll bake up a batch of Aunt Dessy's biscuits for breakfast."

They both chuckled. "What are they?" I asked.

"Your great-aunt Dessy always got her recipes all mixed-up. She could never remember whether it was a cup of flour and a pinch of salt, or a pinch of flour and a cup of salt. So her biscuits were hard as rocks," Aunt Pretty explained.

"No wonder Uncle Jonah didn't have a tooth left in his head," Pa said, and they exploded into laughter, though going without teeth didn't seem too funny to me. "Yep, Dessy's biscuits were downright Wonders," Pa added, and he and my aunt laughed even harder.

"That's not what I mean!" I was getting seriously

annoyed. "I'm talking about things so special, folks would travel all around the world to see them!"

Aunt Pretty put down her crocheting and sighed. "Eben, why *do* you spend so much time thinking about those foreign places?"

"Because someday I'm going to see them," I told her. "I'm going round the world on a tramp steamer, like the fellow who wrote this book."

Aunt Pretty huffed and started crocheting with a vengeance. "Wouldn't that be a scandal! Leaving your pa alone with all this work. Leaving the farm to go to rack and ruin."

"Eben's free to lead his own life, once he's grown up," Pa said. "If the farm doesn't suit him."

I stared at the barn for a spell. "Why do all the barns in Sassafras Springs look the same?" To this day, I don't know why I was in such a complaining frame of mind, but I was. "Why isn't there a round one? Or a blue one? Or one with a tower?"

Aunt Pretty's crochet hook hung in midair. "A round blue barn with a tower. Now I've heard everything. What would people think?"

"Maybe they'd think Sassafras Springs is a place worth seeing, instead of just passing us by," I told her.

"Sassafras Springs is as good a place to live as any I've heard of." Aunt Pretty's voice was firm. "We'd look silly with a pyramid out in our cornfield."

"Just think, Pretty, we could charge folks to see it," Pa joked. "You could sell the tourists lemonade and your good apple pie."

My aunt laughed. I did not.

Pa eyeballed his whittling stick again. "That Egypt looks to be a mighty dry place. I wonder how they grow the crops to live on."

"They've done fine for all these years," I snapped back.

A lopsided moon popped up in the dusky sky, but it didn't shed light on any Wonders.

"Maybe our buildings are lacking in originality," Pa admitted. "Still, I can't believe there aren't a few Wonders around here somewhere. Maybe a little smaller than that pyramid, so's you haven't noticed yet."

I didn't mean to sigh as giant a sigh as I did right then. The light was fading fast, and Aunt Pretty's crochet hook was flying like fury.

Pa stared out at the farm with a faraway look in his eyes. "Annie May always wanted to go up to Silver Peak, Colorado, to see Cousin Molly and her husband,

Eli. She wanted to see a real, honest-to-goodness tall mountain, the kind with snow on top. I sure wish I'd have taken her."

I swallowed the lump of sorrow I felt whenever Ma's name came up. Sal got up and pressed her chin on my knee.

We all sat silent, even Aunt Pretty, until Pa asked, "Does that book tell what a Wonder really is?"

I thumbed through the pages, back to the introduction. "Here it is. It says, 'a marvel; that which arouses awe, astonishment, surprise, or admiration.'"

Pa scratched his cheek with the dull side of his knife. "I've seen one or two things to admire around here. Maybe if you put out a little effort, you would too."

I closed the book and leaned back on both elbows. "But what's the point?"

"I just think there's no use searching the world for Wonders when you can't see the marvels right under your own nose."

"Amen," said Aunt Pretty.

It wasn't enough to satisfy me, not in the mood I was in. "Just what marvels are you talking about?"

Pa stood up and started pacing around, rubbing

the back of his neck the way he always did when he was pondering something important.

"Eben, I have a deal for you," he finally announced. "You find yourself Seven Wonders right here in Sassafras Springs, and I'll buy you a ticket to go see Molly and Eli and that mountain!"

I almost fell off the porch. So did Aunt Pretty.

"All by himself?" she asked, rolling her eyes. "An eleven-year-old boy staying with folks who are practically strangers out there in the wilderness?"

Pa ignored her. "Of course, like you say, you probably can't find seven amazing things in all of Sassafras Springs, but you could try."

My mind was racing. "A train ticket? When?"

"Reckon there's time right before harvest."

"Can I enter this contest?" Aunt Pretty asked.

"The deal's between me and the boy." Pa rose from his chair and disappeared into the house.

"Colorado." Aunt Pretty shook her head. "Why, I would have been tickled pink just to go over to St. Clair when I was a girl."

I've never been able to picture my aunt as a girl. Her real name, Purity, got shortened to "Pretty" years ago. The name stuck, though she'd added a few pounds over the years. Pleasingly plump, as she said. Pa always told her she was still in her prime. "You're a fine figure of a woman, little sister," he'd say. That made Aunt Pretty blush every time.

The door squealed as Pa came back outside and handed me a pad of paper. "You can keep track of your Wonders here."

"How long do I have?"

"Seven days seems fair," said Pa, settling back down. "Long as it took for God to create this world and take a day off."

"A Wonder a day? I don't know." At that moment, seven of anything sounded like a lot. Especially since if Sassafras Springs had Wonders, they hadn't showed up so far.

Still, I could already hear that train whistle calling, could already see those tracks pointing toward the white-capped mountains of Colorado.

"I'll start tomorrow."

I guess Columbus said something like that once, only he said it in Italian.

## Day One
# I Go Searching

The next morning didn't seem that different from any other Wednesday in July. Up at first light, I stepped out on the porch and stared across the yard, out at the fields, the orchard, and beyond. I didn't see a thing that would impress an Egyptian.

I fed Murph and Pat while Pa milked Mabel and Myrt. Then we harnessed the horses and headed straight to the fields. By that year, which was 1923, a few farmers had tractors, but Pa said the problem with machines was when you said whoa, they kept on going. Unlike Murph and Pat.

I knew it'd be foolish to look for Wonders on our own land. I'd been up and down the rows of corn and beans so often, I knew every clump of dirt.

While I weeded, I did come up with a plan of how to start my search. When you're plowing or mowing, you start at the beginning of one row and go all the way to the end. Then you move up the next row to the end, and so on. That's how I'd go looking for Wonders: up one country lane and down the next, until I'd covered all of Sassafras Springs. Seven days should be enough time.

Still, I wasn't convinced I'd find anything awe-inspiring.

In the late afternoon, Pa gave me a break from chores—that alone would count as a Wonder in my book, though I didn't say it out loud. He might have called off the deal altogether, and I wasn't about to let that happen.

I stuffed the tablet in my back pocket, and Sal and I walked out to Yellow Dog Road. That's what they call the wide strip of dirt that goes straight down the middle of Sassafras Springs. In winter it's as slick as glass. In spring and fall it turns to mush. In summer it's plain yellow dirt, so dusty I could taste it.

"I've got a plan, Sal," I announced. Sal wasn't much interested in plans. She let her nose lead her where it would—usually toward the nearest squirrel or rabbit.

Across the road I could see a group of farms up on a rocky ridge midway up Redhead Hill. There were a couple more in the valley below. On our side of the road was our place, three other farms, and the Community Church.

If you went all the way down Yellow Dog Road, you'd connect with the County Road, a two-lane highway that brought the occasional traveler or salesman to town. My best friend Jeb and I used to sit at that crossroads when we were younger, waiting for something interesting to come along, like an automobile or a circus wagon.

Once, when we were eight, a city fellow in a straw hat and red suspenders stopped and asked us directions. He was traveling downstate to attend the College of Mines and Metallurgy. Didn't that sound like a fine place—folks sitting around studying gold and silver all day! Jeb and I talked about it all summer, rolling that name around: College of Mines and Metallurgy.

At the crossroads of the County Road and Yellow Dog lay a scattering of stores and houses. It wasn't much of a town, though there was talk of building a community hall. Just talk, Pa said.

On the other side of the County Road ran Liberty Creek. It was a good place to swim, skip stones, fish, or float a small boat—if you watched out for rocks and didn't mind the occasional snake. Wild sassafras grew along the banks, and upstream a spring fed the creek. It's not too hard to figure out how our town got its name.

Standing there in the middle of Yellow Dog Road, I could see plenty of land but nothing more wonderful than barns and silos.

"Maybe we need some company," I told Sal. "No use doing this all alone."

We walked down to the Austins' to see if Jeb wanted to come along. Even though his family's farm was next door to ours, it was still a hike to get there. Dusty, their big brown dog, ran up to greet Sal and me and led us to the vegetable patch, where Jeb was riding herd on a whole pack of Austins.

He had four younger sisters and four younger brothers. The babies were inside with their ma and the oldest girl, Maggie, but the rest of them hung all over Jeb, as usual. You hardly ever saw him without a brother clinging to his leg, a sister riding piggyback, and another one tugging at his back pocket. Fortunately, Jeb was good-natured.

"Want to come searching with me?" I asked him.

"Looking for trouble? I got some here," said Jeb, ruffling Flo's hair.

"Hi, Eben," she said with a giggle. "Got any candy?"

Before I could answer, Charlie lunged for Sal, yelling "Doggie!" She escaped his grasp in the nick of time.

Don't get me wrong—I like Jeb's brothers and sisters. But whenever I tried to tell Jeb he was lucky, he'd say, "Take as many of 'em as you want."

"I was hoping you and me could go searching for Wonders. Like the Seven Wonders of the World. Remember? In geography?"

Jeb grabbed Fred's overalls just in time to keep him from mowing down a tomato plant.

"Nothing like that around here," he said. "You got your work cut out for you."

"If I can find Seven Wonders in Sassafras Springs, I'll get to go to Colorado on the train."

Jeb let out a low whistle. "By yourself?"

I nodded, just as Bessie burst into tears because Joey was dangling a fat worm in her face.

"Maybe tomorrow," said Jeb, picking up Bessie. "I kind of have my hands full today."

I trudged back toward the road with Sal at my heels.

"Looks like we're on our own," I told her. She wagged her tail, grateful-like.

We took the side road off Yellow Dog and headed up the hill, past fields tall with corn, aiming toward the farthest side of the ridge. "I guess this is the beginning, girl," I told Sal.

Well, the two of us walked and climbed and searched and explored but we didn't see anything out of the ordinary. At this rate, at the end of seven days I'd have an empty tablet and a dog full of cockleburs.

I sat down and tried to pick the ornery stickers out of Sal's fur and she licked my hand in thanks.

"Well, girl, guess we better keep on looking." Then I remembered part of a verse I'd heard last week in Sunday school. "He that seeketh findeth."

That sounded encouraging. I recalled another part of that chapter said, "Ask, and it shall be given you."

Maybe finding Wonders would require some asking, though speaking up did not come naturally to me, as Aunt Pretty liked to point out.

I craned my neck and glimpsed the very top of Redhead Hill, trying to imagine how much higher Silver Peak Mountain would be.

"Come on, girl," I told Sal, as I stood up and brushed off the seat of my trousers. "Let's go seek and find some Wonders."

The farthest farmhouse belonged to Mr. and Mrs. Orville Payne. Once a month or so I saw Mrs. Almeta Payne in our parlor, along with half a dozen other ladies from the church sewing circle. How their needles kept up with their tongues was a mystery to me, but I thought I'd call on Mrs. Payne and see if she had anything astonishing to show me.

There were two windows on the front of the Payne house, one on each side of the door. With the shades pulled halfway down, they looked like a pair of sleepy eyes. I took a deep breath and knocked. It was dead quiet inside.

I thought Mrs. Payne might be out back and went to check. As I rounded the side of the house, I practically ran smack into Mr. Payne, and he wasn't pleased to see me. Neither was his huge dog, who bared his yellow teeth at Sal. She stood her ground but kept quiet, as the Payne dog was double her size. Sal was brave but she wasn't stupid.

Orville Payne was a tall man—so tall that when I looked up at him I could see clear inside his nostrils. They were flaring like an angry bull's.

"What you doing here?" he asked in a gravelly voice.

"Why, looking for Mrs. Payne. It's me, Eben McAllister."

He frowned and blew his red nose on a ragged bandanna. "Why ain't you home with your pa?"

"Well, sir, I'm looking around Sassafras Springs for a Wonder. You know, like a Wonder of the World?"

Mr. Payne spit on the ground. "More like you're nosing around to see if anybody has anything worth stealing. Now you git out of here and stay out. I don't want boys like you snooping around my house. Go on, now!"

He didn't have to tell me twice. As Sal and I hightailed it out of there, my heart was leaping around in my chest.

Folks in Sassafras Springs were usually friendly enough, but they expected their neighbors to mind their own business, which did not include asking about Wonders.

When we were out of Orville Payne's sight, I stopped to catch my breath. I was ready to give up and go home. I decided I'd try keeping my eyes open for Wonders while keeping my mouth shut.

On the way back down the hill, I rounded a bend and saw somebody waving at me, friendly-like. I waved back.

When Sal and I got closer, I saw that the arm was really the sleeve of a dress hanging on a wash line along with shirts and "unmentionables," as Aunt Pretty called underwear. They were outside the house where Mrs. Pritchard, my Sunday school teacher, lived.

Just then, Mrs. Pritchard herself stepped out from behind the wash and waved. She was small and round: round face, round curls, big round flowers on her dress. Neat as a pin, Aunt Pretty would say.

"Is that you, Eben?" she called.

Sal raced ahead but I was in no hurry. The house was so small, I don't know how the Pritchards raised a family in it. Aunt Pretty said Mrs. Pritchard had no business putting on airs and graces when her house was no better than anybody else's. Not that anyone would know, since it was about as hard to get invited into the Pritchards' house as to be admitted through the Pearly Gates.

I didn't exactly expect to find a Statue of Zeus hiding behind the picket fence.

"Howdy," I said when I finally reached the wash line, feeling kind of shy. It didn't seem right to be standing next to my Sunday school teacher's bloomers. She asked how Pa was and how Aunt Pretty was and how I was, all the while pulling down sun-dried pillowcases and folding them.

"We're all fine, ma'am."

Mrs. Pritchard liked to get right to the point. "Well, what can I do for you?"

It was Mrs. Pritchard who'd taught me that Bible verse about asking and receiving, so I took a deep breath and summoned up a chunk of courage.

"Maybe you could help me find something, ma'am. You see, I made a bet with Pa."

"I do not approve of gambling." Mrs. Pritchard's voice was firm. "Neither does the Good Book." The woman looked harmless, but one time she caught Albert Bowie making faces behind her back during class. She yanked his ear hard until he cried "uncle." Albert's acted like a genuine angel ever since, at least on Sunday mornings.

"Not a gambling kind of bet," I explained. "I'm trying to find a Wonder here in Sassafras Springs. A man-made Wonder. Something amazing and awe-inspiring." I stopped to draw a breath. "Like the pyramids—but it doesn't have to be that big."

"What a funny idea," Mrs. Pritchard said. "I think you are on a fool's errand looking for Wonders around here! Better you go home and study that Sunday school lesson. Book of Mark, Chapter four, Verse thirty. The Parable of the Mustard Seed. Study that, Eben, instead of bothering folks for Wonders."

Clutching the pillowcases close to her chest, she walked toward her house.

"See you on Sunday," I called to her. Sal had already beat me to the road.

I hated to think of that train to Colorado leaving the station without me, but I didn't hold out a lot of hope. My mind was fixed on snow-covered mountains, so Sal heard her calling before I did.

"Come back, Eben McAllister! Come on back here!"

Suddenly Mrs. Pritchard was racing down the road after me.

"I just remembered something! Don't know how it slipped my mind." Mrs. Pritchard was a mite plump, so she was breathing hard by the time she caught up with me. "I don't have some fancy pyramid. But if you want to see the greatest Wonder of this world or any other, well, just follow me. Don't dawdle, now!"

She marched to her house like a soldier, and you can bet I followed her. I didn't want to get my ear pulled.

"Not you," I told Sal when we got to the door. Sal's not one to get her feelings hurt. She lay down in the cool shade outside as I stepped through the doorway. Wouldn't Aunt Pretty be surprised to know I was being invited into the Pritchard house! Wouldn't she like to know every last detail!

Mrs. Pritchard went straight to a tall cabinet, opened a drawer, and picked up something wrapped in tissue paper. "I haven't shown this to anyone in years. But you asked for a Wonder. Eben, you'll never see more of a Wonder than this." She carefully peeled back the paper.

The shriveled-up face staring at me sent shivers up my spine. I knew it was an applehead doll, but it reminded me of the shrunken head I'd seen in my exploring book.

Aunt Pretty told me that when she was growing up, the only dolls country girls had were made of rags, dried apples, or clothespins. Mrs. Pritchard's doll had yellow yarn hair, an old-fashioned dress, and two hollows carved out of the leathery apple for eyes. Why anybody—even a girl—would take a fancy to a doll was beyond me, but this one was something special. This one was ugly as sin.

"I see you don't fully appreciate Miss Zeldy," said Mrs. Pritchard. "Still, I promise you, this doll is a Wonder, formed by the hand of man with a spirit that goes beyond anything man can understand."

She cradled the doll and sat down. "Only a doll, you may be thinking, Eben. An old woman's doll at that. However, once you hear Miss Zeldy's story, even a young man like you will sit up and take notice."

I was already taking notice, especially when Mrs. Pritchard held Zeldy on her knee like some hideous child. I half expected the doll to start talking. I felt those hollowed-out eyes staring right through me and the hairs on the back of my neck tingled.

Mrs. Pritchard pointed to a hard green sofa opposite her. "Sit down now, Eben McAllister, and pay attention to what I have to say," she ordered me.

So I sat. Because when folks in Sassafras Springs start to tell a story, it's likely to take a while.

# Mrs. Pritchard's Story

## Miss Zeldy's Message

*I grew up over on Lead Ridge. My papa was the preacher there. You didn't know I was a preacher's daughter, did you? Papa was an educated man, been to Seminary. He read books, even though we didn't have two pennies to rub together, ministering to the poor miners. We thought we were as rich as kings, the way Mama sewed and cooked. Papa was handy too, carving up tops and other toys for us. Most years at Christmas, we were lucky enough to get an orange, a peppermint stick, and a new pair of socks or a handkerchief embroidered with Mama's fine stitching—more than most. Not like you young people today who get store-bought gifts.*

In spite of Mama's good care I was a sickly child

and always small for my age. One year, when I was about six, I guess, a cough took hold of me and wouldn't let go. Mama tried everything: red alder bark tea, hot water with onion juice. Once Mama even made Papa get me a little whiskey to drink in hot water. It would have been a scandal if his congregation found out, but they were desperate to cure me. How people get to liking the taste of spirits, I'll never know. And I certainly hope you resist that temptation!

Anyway, Mama'd rub my chest with a mixture of kerosene, turpentine, camphor, and lard. Still, my cough got stronger and my body got weaker. My folks didn't think I'd last through the winter. Until I took sick, I slept upstairs with my sisters where it was cold as the devil's heart. So Mama fixed me a bed downstairs in front of the stove, trying to keep me warm, and Papa carried me wherever I needed to go.

Around Thanksgiving the coughing got worse. At Thanksgiving dinner after Pa said grace, Ma choked up and got tears in her eyes.

"I don't feel as thankful as I might," she said.

"Be thankful she's still here, Libby," Pa told her.

I knew he was talking about me.

A while later they got the doctor to come. He had the sad look of a man who's given up. When he took Mama and Papa aside to talk, he shook his head, like there was nothing he could do.

"The fever's taken hold. If only she'd been stronger to start with," I heard him say. "She's in the Lord's hands now."

Sure enough, I had a fever that left me shaking one minute and burning up the next. In between I dreamed that I was floating in the air, right up near the rafters of the room.

On Christmas Eve, like in a dream, I heard Papa tell Mama to pray with him that I'd make it to Christmas morning. It was a rough night, and Mama never left my side a minute. The next day when I woke up, the first thing I laid eyes on was my stocking. Peeking up over the top was my very own baby doll. My precious Miss Zeldy.

Oh, and there was a tiny chair and bed for her, carved by Papa. Mama had made her all kinds of hats and aprons and such. Pretty things—even a coat with a real fur collar. I thought Miss Zeldy was the most beautiful doll in the world. Little did I know what power she held.

I cuddled her and kissed her. Papa teased me by calling me Little Mama. I liked that. I thought of Miss Zeldy as my own baby, as much as any of my six children were later on. That's the gospel truth.

That night at bedtime I heard Mama tell Papa, "She made it through the day! That doll has worked a miracle."

Of course, he reminded her that only the Lord can work a miracle. Mama said she didn't care who made the miracle, she only cared that I was alive. I'd never heard Mama talk back to Papa like that before.

I rocked Miss Zeldy and tucked her in her bed next to mine. I left a thimble full of water next to her tiny bed, like my Mama left a cup of water by my bed. And later, when my fever rose and I felt that floating feeling again, I reached over and held on to Miss Zeldy.

No matter how much I loved my doll, I still kept getting weaker and weaker. When Mama put a piece of flannel cloth on my chest with the kerosene and turpentine remedy on it, I made her put one on Miss Zeldy, too. Every night I put out her thimble of water and kissed her good night.

Sometime between Christmas and the New Year, the doctor came to call, and he still had that sad look.

"Her heart is weak," I heard him tell Mama and Papa. "Keep praying, but you'd best prepare for the worst."

It was odd, because even though I could hear them talking, I felt like I was floating on a cloud above them. What they said didn't seem to have anything to do with me.

Floating felt nice. I was drifting farther and farther away, like I was gliding up to heaven. I'd always liked to watch the barn swallows soar and swoop across the sky. That's what I was doing, soaring and swooping, flying farther and farther away from Earth.

Then I heard a voice. Although I'd never heard it before, I knew right away who that voice belonged to.

"Little Mama, I'm thirsty! Little Mama, I want something to drink!" the voice called.

I didn't like being interrupted. I wanted to float forever. But that funny voice kept calling me.

"Wake up, Little Mama, I need a drink. Give me a drink now, Mama, please!"

She was thirsty, you see? And I had to be a good mother like my own mama was. I had to stop floating and come back down to Earth and get Miss Zeldy a drink. I was as certain of it then as I am now.

When I opened my eyes, her thimble of water had tipped over and was bone dry.

I sat straight up in bed, like I'd never been sick, and from that minute on I got better and better.

The doctor said I was just out of my head until the fever broke. Papa called it a miracle and preached about it in church. When I tried to tell them I'd heard Miss Zeldy, they smiled and said it was the sickness.

"Why won't anyone believe it was my doll?" I moaned in frustration.

"I believe you," Mama said. She kissed me good night and she kissed Zeldy too. I've never forgotten that she believed that this humble doll came to life for a few sweet moments to save my life.

Yes, young man, to this day I know I wouldn't have ever awakened in the glory of this world again if she hadn't called for that water. I wouldn't have married Hank Pritchard, raised six healthy children, and taught Bible stories to young folks like you.

The doll's a Wonder of the world—maybe not of this world but of the next one. You write that down, Eben McAllister. When I tell you this is a Wonder, you'd better listen. Because just as miracles were

worked with loaves and fishes, one was worked through this doll. If anybody says it's not true, you have them come talk to me.

———

There was no arguing with Mrs. Pritchard when she took that tone. I picked up my tablet and began to write. Even though her story was peculiar, by jiggers, it amazed me, and it might even get me to Colorado.

Even so, I knew that I couldn't ever sit in Sunday school again without seeing that shriveled-up face and those hollow eyes. I decided not to think about it for a while.

Instead I flew back down the hill with Sal at my heels as if there was no such thing as gravity to hold me to the earth.

Day Two
# Jeb Joins In

"Did you bring us one of those big statues for the yard?" Aunt Pretty asked at dinner that night.

I had no idea what she was talking about.

"She means a Wonder, son," said Pa.

I wasn't ready to share that crazy doll story, not yet. I knew Aunt Pretty would want to know all about the curtains and fancy doodads at the Pritchards', but I hadn't noticed a thing but the doll.

"I'm going to wait and see what I've got at the end of the week," I told them.

"Oh, and you just know I hate to wait," Aunt Pretty fussed.

Pa changed the subject. "Mighty fine eats. Eben

may sail the seven seas, but he'll never find as fine a cook as you, Pretty."

I looked down at the plate of ham, boiled beans and fluffy biscuits. I knew a peach pie was waiting on the windowsill. "Yessir," I agreed.

For an instant I felt a pang, picturing myself in Tokyo or Timbuktu, craving one of my aunt's peach pies.

Aunt Pretty said, "Oh, go on now," and plopped a big heap of beans on my plate. "Have some seconds."

I didn't want to disappoint her, no sir, so I had my second helping and put Timbuktu clean out of my mind.

When you're weeding corn, up one row and down the next, you have a lot of time to think. So all Thursday morning I thought of that faraway mountain in Silver Peak, Colorado. The more weeds I dug up, the higher that mountain got. With one Wonder under my belt, I was itching to go in search of more, but Pa was working extra hard and I didn't have the heart to ask to take time off.

Around half past three, Pa stopped abruptly. "That's enough, Eben," he said. "I won't be needing you till milking time."

I didn't waste a second. I splashed the dust off my face at the pump and took a nice long drink. I checked that my paper and pencil were in my back pocket and headed for Yellow Dog Road with Sal tagging along. When I reached the edge of the Austins' farm, Jeb came racing toward me, kicking up a cloud of dust.

"Wait up! I'm coming with you!"

I looked around. "Where's the rest of the brood?"

"Maggie said she'd watch them, but I've got to dry the dishes tonight in her place." Jeb didn't want to waste time talking about chores. "Any luck with those Wonders?"

I thought his big brown eyes would pop right out of his face when I told him about Mrs. Pritchard. "A doll? What kind of a Wonder is that?"

"A doll that saved somebody's life!" I told him. "I think that's a Wonder, even if it is a peculiar one. You got any better ideas?"

Jeb shook his head. "Naw. I've never seen anything special, except that three-legged cow my grandpa used to have."

"That wasn't man-made," I told him.

"Nope. It was a freak of nature. That's what

Grandpa said." Jeb stooped to pick up a hedge apple and pitched it across the road.

"I'm going all along the ridge first." I told him about Orville Payne.

"Whoo-ee," said Jeb. "You're lucky he didn't aim his shotgun at you. He'd just as soon shoot you as look at you."

I hadn't thought about firearms before. "At least I got something."

"A *doll* story." Jeb reached down for another hedge apple. This time he pulled his arm way back and sent it arching high into the air. "Hey, if you're looking for something special, we should go down to the Saylor house. A rich person is more likely to have a Wonder than a poor one. Maybe two or three."

The Saylor place, right in town, was the only house in Sassafras Springs that had curlicues and fancy trim, and a fine porch that curved all around the side, not to mention a big sleeping porch upstairs.

The Saylors had money, something in short supply everywhere else in town. They owned the feed store, which also dealt in farm equipment. Farmers could do without new clothes, indoor plumbing, and even full bellies, but they couldn't do without farm equipment. That's why the Saylors had the biggest house in Sassafras Springs. And a Ford motorcar in the driveway to boot. Some farmers, like Pa, had old pickup trucks, but the Saylors were the only folks who had a car just for riding around in.

"I don't know about this," I told Jeb as we gingerly walked up the front steps. There was a window in the door with colored glass in it, put together to look like a rose. "Mrs. Saylor might not cotton to boys like us calling on her."

Before I had time to talk myself out of knocking, the door swung open and there was Mrs. Saylor, dressed all in pink, with a big smile on her face.

"Hello, young men. I thought I heard footsteps."

"Howdy, ma'am," I mumbled.

Mrs. Saylor was young—much younger than Mr. Saylor—and her soft brown hair was piled high on her head. "What can I do for you?"

Jeb just stared at her like the cat got his tongue, but I managed to blurt out something about looking for Wonders.

"Maybe you'd better come in," she said.

The inside of the house was so full of furniture and pictures, rugs and lacy things, that it looked like a store. It wasn't the place for the likes of Jeb and me.

"I'm not sure I have what you're looking for." Mrs. Saylor furrowed her brow. "But I'll have a think."

She had us sit on a sofa decorated with roses— I guess they were her favorite flowers.

"You wait here and I'll be right back."

Jeb had yet to say one word. He just sat and stared.

After a while I heard the rustling of her skirts, and Mrs. Saylor came back carrying a red satin box.

"I suppose this is our best bet," she said, sitting in a fuzzy blue chair across from us. She carefully opened it and pulled out a long strand of pinkish-colored pearls.

"These pearls belonged to Mr. Saylor's great-grandmother. Aren't they lovely?"

She waited for some kind of reaction so I said, "Yes, ma'am," while Jeb just nodded.

She reached in again and pulled out a circle of small green beads. "And this is genuine jade from China, boys. Isn't that a Wonder?"

I leaned in to look at the jade and mumbled something about it being nice, though the green glass beads Aunt Pretty won at the county fair last year looked just as pretty and sparkled a whole lot more.

Next Mrs. Saylor pulled out a brooch, with the outline of a lady in it, all carved in white. "And this is my grandmother's hand-carved cameo."

Jeb and I made admiring noises. "Who did the carving?" I asked.

"Oh, a jewelry maker in Paris," she said in a tone that let me know that French jewelry makers were a lot better than the ones in Missouri.

"Do you think these are Wonders?" she asked, biting her lip. Mrs. Saylor surely aimed to please.

"Yes, ma'am," I told her. "The very finest."

Mrs. Saylor looked relieved. She picked up another box—a cardboard box in the shape of a heart—off the table next to her. "Have a chocolate, boys. All the way from St. Louis."

She lifted the lid, uncovering rows of chocolates: round, square, and heart-shaped ones. "The round ones are cream-filled, the square ones are solid chocolate, and the heart-shaped ones have nuts," she explained.

It only took a few seconds for my hand to land on a square chocolate while Jeb picked out a cream-filled one. We didn't know what to do next until Mrs. Saylor said, "I believe I'll have a heart-shaped one."

She popped the chocolate in her mouth. "Go ahead, boys," she urged us. So we ate ours, chewing in silence, and oh, I'd never tasted chocolate like that before.

There was nothing left to do but thank Mrs. Saylor, say our farewells, and get out. As we hurried down the steps, Mr. Saylor arrived home, wearing a three-piece suit and a big-city hat.

"What did those rascals want?" I heard him ask his wife at the door.

"Oh, they were just looking for something," she said. "I gave them chocolates."

"You are too soft-hearted, Lily," he said. "But that's what makes you so special."

"Did you see those pearls? They must be worth a fortune! And those stones from China too!" Jeb exclaimed once we were down the road apiece.

"They were fine, but they were no Wonders," I told him.

Jeb looked like I'd just told him the sky was red instead of blue. "Why, nothing in Sassafras Springs is worth what that jewelry's worth," he said.

"I know, but those three things together aren't worth one doll like Mrs. Pritchard's. All you can do with a string of pearls is hang them around your neck. I think I need to go back to where I left off yesterday."

"If you're going back up the ridge, the next stop after the Pritchards' is Cully Pone's. If you go there, you'll be plenty sorry."

"Why?"

"'Cause that Cully is crazy. Everybody knows it," said Jeb. "You go over there and you won't live to see your mountain."

Cully Pone *was* a bit odd, I agreed. But he was harmless, according to Pa. Jeb did not agree.

"Has he got a gun?" I wondered.

"Who knows? He's got wild eyes. And he holds up his trousers with a rope."

What Jeb said was true. I could skip Cully's place, but I'd kick myself hard if I ended up missing a Wonder.

"If that's the next place on the ridge, then I'm going there. Come with me. There's safety in numbers," I told Jeb.

Jeb stopped in the road and turned to me. "I'll walk up there with you," he said. "But I'm not going in that house."

"Deal," I agreed.

"Who's that?" Cully shouted as we approached his shack. Jeb and Sal both hung back when he lurched toward us, ax in hand. His eyes lit up as he raised the ax up above his shoulder.

I closed my eyes so as not to watch my own head being chopped off. When nothing happened, I opened them, just as Cully rested the ax back on his shoulder and showed off his four teeth in a wide grin.

"Boys, is it? Thought you was the tax collector. Haven't had a caller in a dog's age. Happy to have you," he said in a loud voice. Cully tended to shout. "Don't know why more folks don't stop by."

Cully Pone was a string bean of a man. That bit of rope couldn't keep his trousers from drooping dangerously low, and the moths had made quite a meal out of his felt hat.

My mouth was dry as a bone, but I managed to explain what I was looking for. To my surprise, he didn't hesitate a tick when I told him what I wanted.

"Yes, indeedy, I got a Wonder," he said as if somebody asked him for one every day. "Yessirree."

He left his ax on the stump he'd been hacking away at and motioned for us to follow him into the house. I had never been inside and neither had anybody else I knew. I wasn't anxious to go in now, because Cully's place—no more than a shack— leaned considerably to the right.

Cully made his living by doing handyman work. The trouble was, not many people wanted to hire a handyman whose own house was about to cave in. He might not have noticed, but everyone else in Sassafras Springs did.

"I'll give it a year," I'd heard Pa tell Aunt Pretty

once. I quickly tried to remember if a year or more had passed since I'd heard him say it.

On the other hand a Wonder is a Wonder, and one more Wonder would take me one step closer to that mountain. So I followed him.

When I glanced back at Jeb, he rolled his eyes as if to say, "When hell freezes over." I figured if I was going to the Nile or the Amazon, I'd have to take a few chances. Against my better judgment, I forced myself to step inside. Sal trotted along behind me and Cully didn't object.

Near the door sat a huge chair covered with a pile of tattered quilts. There was an old potbellied stove in the corner and a bunch of wooden crates that Cully used for furniture.

What caught my eye was a bookcase set dead in the middle of the room. It reached all the way to the ceiling. Or I should say, the ceiling sagged down and rested on top of the bookcase. The wood was split and warped and the shelves leaned at crazy angles. Every inch was covered with useless items: bent fishing poles, dusty pop bottles, what might have been an ancient coconut, and a rusty mousetrap with a piece of cheese so old and dry, even the hungriest rat would pass it by.

Cully walked up to the bookcase and patted it, proudlike.

"Yep. Here's a guaranteed Wonder of the county. Even the state. And maybe even a Wonder of the whole doggone world."

"You're talking about the bookcase?"

"Yessirree, it's a bookcase," Cully bellowed. "My prized possession. Had it since I was a boy. Never read me a book, but by jiggers,

I have a bookcase. The doggone doggonedest bookcase you ever did hear of, too."

Cully dropped into the chair and patted a crate for me to sit on. I didn't have time to worry about whether the roof would fall in or whether the crate would give way.

Cully Pone was starting his story.

# Cully Pone's Story

## The Rainmaker's Revenge

*This here bookcase once held the secrets of the universe, and it saved a couple of lives to boot. You probably never heard of Henry Upton, but folks up in Garnerville did. That's in Garner County on the Garner River . . . about fifty miles north of here. Say, they like the name Garner there, don't they?*

They had themselves a grand old drought when I was a boy. One year was dry. The second year was drier. The third year, there wasn't enough rain to wet a postage stamp. The famous Garner County corn was as shriveled as that dead old tree stump out front, and the river had no more water in it than you could squeeze out of a rock. Things looked bad for the farmers, I'll tell you that.

Around that time a fellow called Henry Upton moved to town, and nobody'd seen the likes of him before. He wore a genuine top hat, like Honest Abe Lincoln—he was president once, you know. Some said Upton was a professor. Some said he was a traveling magician. Some said he was the son of one of the richest families back East. He moved into a cabin up on Rooster Ridge, the highest point in Garner County. Brought along a wagonload of fancy furniture—crystal lamps, horsehair sofas, and such. And he brought this here bookcase. Might have looked fancier then, but it's the same one.

The shelves were crammed with books. And the spaces where there weren't any books were filled with jars and bottles of smelly crystals and cloudy liquids. He didn't work the land, just read all day long. "Uppity" Upton, they called him from the start.

Yessirree, one day this Uppity Upton took himself down to the Garnerville town hall and walked right into the town board meeting like he was invited, which he was not. He stood there with a big smile on his face and made the board an offer: He promised to make it rain on Garner County. If he did, they'd have to pay him five hundred dollars an inch! He guaranteed them ten inches for five thousand dollars.

Those board members thought he was funny in the head. Even the mayor broke down and laughed. "What are ya gonna do, Uppity? A rain dance?"

Henry Upton had long gangly arms and legs and a round middle, so the idea of him dancing had the whole town board laughing. Uppity stayed calm and waited until they quieted down, then he said he was going to use sci-en-ti-fic methods.

That made the board members hoot and holler to beat the band. Uppity raised his arms to quiet them down. "You only pay me if you get results," he told them. "You can't lose on the deal."

Whoa, Nellie, that got them to thinking. Some of them were ready to sign him right up. The mayor argued that even if it did rain, there was no way Upton could prove it was because of him and not the Lord God Almighty. Uppity got *real* uppity and said, "Apparently the Lord God Almighty has not seen fit to make it rain around here so far. How much longer are you willing to wait?"

Yee-haw! That got the Garnerville town-board folks thinking. Some said they couldn't afford to let their corn crops wither away. Others said that it was wrong to fool with nature. Some said Upton was a crackpot—said it right to his face! The place was in an uproar, and Upton's face grew purple. "Does this mean you're turning down my deal?" he asked.

The mayor stood up and looked at Upton eyeball to eyeball. "You're dadburned right we're turning you and your harebrained scheme down!" And with that, Upton left, mad enough to bust his fancy gold buttons.

The next morning he built a platform on Rooster Ridge. He built a brick fireplace with a huge chimney pointing straight up at the cloudless sky. And over the platform, he built a roof to protect the fire from rain. Which there was none, of course. It was like a house without walls.

Next he built a fire and started pouring strange, smelly powders onto the flames. Smoke the colors of the rainbow rose up out of that fire and kept on rising all the way up to the sky! Yes indeedy, rose halfway to heaven.

The folks around Garnerville were watching every move he made. They saw him take a cot out on the platform and some blankets and, by Jehoshaphat, he slept there all night, getting up to add his secret potion every few hours. That fire never went out, morning to night, night to morning.

Exactly forty-eight hours after the fires began, the clouds rolled in over Garner County. Those clouds opened up and poured down rain. It didn't rain cats and dogs; it rained cows and horses . . . lions and tigers . . . boy, it rained elephants and giraffes!

The Garner River began to rise. The seed corn began to sprout. They were celebrating in the kitchen of every farmhouse for fifty miles.

Uppity gave the town board a bill for the first five inches. And did they pay Uppity? Oh, they talked about it. While the rain gushed down, they chatted. While the Brownstown Bridge washed out, they discussed. While the sprouted seed corn washed away, they argued. While two farmhouses slid into the Garner River, they debated. Meanwhile, Henry Upton kept that fire a-burning night and day, and the rain kept pouring down.

Finally, one day he stopped long enough to trot down to the board meeting—which had been going on for the better part of a week—and demanded his payment in full!

The mayor said, "We never made a deal with you, Upton. Maybe it was going to rain anyway, without your hocus-pocus. We're not paying you a penny."

This time old Uppity didn't argue. He went back to Rooster Ridge and piled on more logs and added more concoctions to that old fire. Purple and blue smoke billowed up from the chimney all day and all evening. When the lightning bolts lit up the sky, people could see Uppity tending that fire like a mother tending her newborn babe.

Five more inches drenched the town that night. Five more inches the next day. Five more by the morning after that.

That night the dam broke and the mayor's house was flooded up to the third floor. He and his family floated their way to the town hall in their bathtub. Half the town board was there already, yowling like a bunch of soggy cats.

For once everybody agreed on one thing: They had to get Uppity to stop his rainmaking. They floated their way to high ground, then slid their way through the mud up to the ridge.

"Stop right there, Upton!" the mayor shouted when they got to Uppity's place. "Have you no mercy?"

Uppity smiled at the mayor, nice as you please. "I'm glad to see you admit that this weather is due to my rainmaking abilities," he told the mayor. "I take it you've brought my payment of five thousand dollars along."

Well, sir, this time the mayor's face turned purple. "I'm not paying you a penny, Upton. Now stop what you're doing, or we'll have to stop you."

"I'll stop," Uppity told them. The mayor and the board members and the sheriff all looked relieved until Upton added, "Pay me ten thousand dollars and I'll stop right now!" Uppity held a jar of crystals over the fire, ready to pour some more on. There was dead silence until—boom!—a huge thunderbolt clattered overhead and the whole kit and caboodle made a beeline out of there.

Uppity kept on mixing and pouring, not stopping to eat or sleep. He was an angry man, ready to get his revenge on Garner County. But he wasn't the only angry man. Down the hill, the mayor gathered together the sheriff and the board and the farmers whose houses had washed away. They all slogged back up to the ridge, mad as wet hens . . . or maybe drenched roosters. Hee-haw!

They carried pitchforks and shovels and any mean-looking thing they could find, and they made a circle around Uppity and his fireplace.

"What's the meaning of this?" Uppity asked.

"You've got five minutes to pack up and get out of here. We want you across that county line tonight," the mayor growled at him.

Uppity argued until the mayor pointed the sharp prongs of his pitchfork at him. "Here's your payment, Upton, if you don't git NOW!"

Well, Upton prepared to git. The sheriff's deputies had already dropped the bookcase onto the wagon along with a trunk full of clothes. The fancy furniture and crystal lamps got left behind. Uppity hopped onto the wagon, gave the reins a slap, and galloped toward the Garner County line.

Halfway across the

Garner River the bridge collapsed, sending Uppity, his wagon, and his horse straight down into the churning waters. The wagon sank like a brick and the horse was swept away. The bookcase landed upside down, and all the books and powders and whatnot were lost. But that old bookcase floated, and Uppity hung on for dear life as the water carried him downstream. He was moving so fast he never noticed when he passed the county line. After a while the rain stopped.

Next morning, as things started to dry up, the sheriff saw those books and bottles floating in the river and figured Upton was floating there too. His body was never found. Leastwise not by anybody in Garner County.

*I* found his body, but it was a living, breathing body. I was just a boy doing some fishing down where the Garner meets Liberty Creek River. I'd never seen the river swelled up so, and I was young enough to think all that rain would bring the fish right to the surface.

My eyes about bugged out of my head when I saw the floating bookcase. As it reached that fork where the rivers meet, the bookcase got caught up on some rocks. Henry Upton sat up and rubbed his eyes. Somewhere in the night he'd flipped the bookcase over and floated the rest of the way lying inside, dozing safe as a chick in its nest. He was a muddy chick, though. Mighty bedraggled.

"Help pull me over, boy. Quick!" Uppity yelled at me. I threw him a big stick, which he used to pull the bookcase closer. He jumped out and waded to shore, dragging the bookcase behind him. When I asked him what'd happened, he said he'd tell me the whole story if I'd find him dry clothes and a hot meal and get him to the nearest train station. Seems Uppity was smart enough to sew his money into his coat. And he had plenty of it too, 'cause he'd earned money all over the U.S.A. making rain for folks in trouble. Folks who paid him plenty, unlike the folks in Garner.

Ma cooked him dinner and Pa gave him some clothes. The man said his rainmaking days were over and he was going to some island where it never rains a drop. He left the bookcase with us, and Pa took him to the train station. And that's the last I ever heard of one Henry Upton. Hee-haw! How's that for a Wonder, boy?

I couldn't tell if the story was over, because Cully kept on chuckling and slapping his knee. When I thought he was finished, I asked him, "Did Upton tell you how he did that rainmaking? You'd make a fortune if you could do it."

"I never even asked," Cully said. "If you'd seen that poor half-drowned critter peering up out of that bookcase, you wouldn't have asked either. I believe in leaving well enough alone, my boy."

Just as I glanced up at his sagging ceiling, it gave out a loud creak. Even calm old Sal jumped up, startled-like. But Cully didn't blink an eye.

"Still, that there's a Wonder, ain't it? A Wonder of the World." Cully stared up at his bookcase as if he was seeing it for the first time. "Held the secrets of the universe, saved a man's life . . . and it's holding up my house today."

"A Wonder," I said. After all, even the Great Pyramid never held up a man's house. I jotted the story down fast, as rain began beating against the windows of the sagging shack.

Poor Jeb was hunkered down under a piece of canvas that covered the woodpile when Sal and I finally came outside.

"Did you get any chocolates?" he called out.

"Something better—a Wonder," I shouted back. "Come on, let's run!"

With Sal in the lead, we raced between the raindrops, back down to Yellow Dog Road.

"It's a wonder you're still alive," Jeb told me along the way.

"You don't know the half of it," I agreed.

## Day Three
# Disappointments

In two days I had two Wonders. It might have just been beginner's luck, but it looked like this wasn't going to be so hard after all.

I'd be on a train soon—my first train ever—chugging away from Sassafras Springs. Or chugging away from St. Clair, since Sassafras Springs didn't have a train station. St. Clair was where folks went for doctoring or banking or big deliveries, like a new wagon or a stove, that could only come by train.

I'd been to St. Clair and it was a fine town, but it just made me hunger to see more. The next town and the next town. If the schoolhouse had been open, I could find the route to Colorado on a map.

There'd be St. Clair, Pine Gap, Garvey City. I couldn't remember what came next.

I'd know soon enough, with just five more Wonders to find. Then I'd be on my way to Colorado.

I hoped the engineer wouldn't be stingy with the whistle.

My aunt had other ideas about the trip, which she made clear that night on the porch. The rain hadn't amounted to more than a few drops, and it was as steamy as the jungles of Borneo—or at least I thought so.

"Cole McAllister, you are encouraging your son to risk his life," Aunt Pretty declared as I finished writing down Cully's story. I'd told her and Pa that Jeb and I had gone to see him, but I didn't let on about Cully's Wonder. "He could have been buried by a collapsing house."

"But he wasn't," said Pa, unperturbed as usual.

"And when do you think Cully Pone last had a bath?" she asked. "Poor dog could have gotten fleas from that man."

Sal cocked her head.

"Aw, and I was thinking of hiring him to do some

work around here." Pa acted serious but I could tell he was teasing.

"You can just think of someone else," my aunt replied. Her crochet hook was racing like greased lightning by then. That woman could crochet anything from a lowly dishcloth to a baby sweater that was soft as a cloud. If a person could crochet a Wonder, she'd be the one to do it. In fact, it wouldn't surprise me at all to find a great pyramid sitting in her lap some day, crocheted in her favorite shades of pink and blue.

That Friday was a scorcher from the minute the sun came up.

"I *would* pick the hottest day of the year to put up fruit." Aunt Pretty said the same thing every year. Sweet-smelling peaches simmered on the stove in one huge pot while canning jars bubbled away in another pot. The kitchen was hot as an oven, and it was just as hot outside.

Pa was already perspiring at seven A.M.

"Do you think it might rain?" I asked, though the cloudless sky didn't give much encouragement.

"Not today," said Pa.

Aunt Pretty brought Pa and me lunch in the field that noon, but she didn't stay to eat with us. "Still putting up peaches," she said. "They probably don't even *grow* those in Colorado. Not that Molly was ever much of a cook."

As I watched her march back to the house, I took a giant gulp of iced tea from the old stone jug.

"Pa, does Aunt Pretty have something against Aunt Molly?" I asked. "She never says anything good about her."

"Molly and Eli are good people, Eben." Pa took a swig of iced tea. "Don't pay any mind to what Pretty says. It's just that she's had her share of sorrows, and she never got a husband of her own."

"How come?" Plenty of women in Sassafras Springs who didn't have good looks or her good qualities had husbands.

"She had admirers, but she fancied Holt Nickerson," Pa recalled. "He bought her apple pie at the church social after competing with two rivals for her attention."

I'd never heard of this Holt Nickerson before. "What happened?"

"Well, sir, Holt was raised by his aunt and uncle, the Culpeppers. His cousin Ned said Holt had quite a habit of sleepwalking. Said they never knew where he'd end up in the morning. Once they found him all curled up in the corn crib and he had no idea how he'd gotten there. Another time they found him leaning against the milk cow, sound asleep, both of them.

"One night Ned heard somebody stirring outside. He hurried downstairs and got to the door just in time to see Holt jump on his horse and ride off in the moonlight, dressed in his long johns, boots, and hat. Ned ran after him, and when he got a glimpse of Holt, he could tell he was asleep with his eyes wide open."

"Didn't he ride after him?"

"'Course he did. Ned rounded up the whole family. They searched high and low, but no one in Sassafras Springs ever saw hide nor hair of Holt again."

I had to sit and think about the story for a bit. "He rode off in his long johns and never came back?" I asked.

"It was a scandal. Your Aunt Pretty pretended not to care, but I could tell she took it hard. I think she was sorry one of those other fellows didn't get her apple pie at the social." Pa paused to chew on some biscuit.

"And her best girlhood friend, Cally, she got herself married and moved to Oregon. Pretty hasn't seen her in years. She has a pack of children and hardly has time to even write anymore."

I suddenly thought of how I'd feel if something happened to Jeb. "What happened to those other fellows that liked Aunt Pretty?" I wondered.

"Married other girls, sad to say. Now, Eben, if you ever mention a word of this to your aunt, there'll be trouble for you."

I promised I wouldn't. But it took a lot of weeding for me to get the picture of Holt Nickerson riding off in his long johns out of my mind.

That afternoon Pa told me I could leave a while, as long as I came back with a sack of sugar for Aunt Pretty by suppertime. And two dozen clothespins, too. That woman really went through clothespins in a hurry. Sometimes I thought she must chew them, like lollipops. My first stop, though, was to drop by Jeb's place to see if he wanted to go searching for Wonders again.

"I've got to work." Jeb plopped down on the ground next to the potatoes. Charlie and Bessie were doing somersaults, while Joey squashed tomato worms as fast as Flo and Fred could pick them off the vines.

"You're a lucky dog to get so much time off," Jeb told me.

"Time off! I just worked so fast I finished early!" Sometimes that Jeb could get under my skin. "Pa said I looked like a cyclone tearing through the fields. And Aunt Pretty said I must have swallowed my lunch whole so I could get out of there."

"I don't see why you're so fired up about this Wonder thing," Jeb said. "You're never really going to see those faraway places."

"Sure I am! Remember that book by Hardy T. Lang that Miss Collins brought in from the lending library in St. Clair? He's that fellow who traveled to all those far-off places, living in jungles with the

69

natives and finding lost temples and sailing on junks and such."

"Junks?"

"Chinese boats," I explained. "Remember the pictures in his book?"

Sometimes I wondered if Jeb paid a lick of attention to the teacher.

Jeb sat back and stuck a long blade of grass between his teeth. "That's okay for somebody in a book, but real folks don't do things like that."

"Hardy T. Lang is a real person. I saw his picture. You did too."

"I'm tired," whined Bess, trying to climb on Jeb's back.

"You got any candy, Eben?" asked Flo.

"Leave us alone, you little beggar." Jeb shooed his sister away, then chewed on his piece of grass awhile before he said, "Must be kind of lonely out there in the world, not knowing anybody. And if you do meet somebody, they don't speak the same language."

"If you and I went together, we'd speak the same language."

Jeb lay back in the grass and stared up at the

sky. "I don't know, Eben. My folks are counting on me to take over the farm some day. It doesn't matter so much for you—you don't have any brothers or sisters. Maybe your pa wants to sell the farm, so he won't need you anyway." He turned on his side, facing toward me. "Maybe I'll go on an adventure with you sometime, but if I do, I'm coming back here."

I know Jeb never meant any harm, but his words stung me like a bee. It wasn't my fault I didn't have brothers and sisters, and Pa never mentioned he wanted to sell the farm. He needed me plenty. Hadn't I worked my tail off for him all morning?

"I've already had enough weeding and plowing to last a lifetime, haven't you?" I asked.

All Jeb said was, "Those natives, they can be dangerous. They have poison darts."

I guess he remembered the book after all.

"I've dealt with Orville Payne and Cully Pone," I told him. "I don't think a few natives will bother me any more than them."

I stood up. To tell the truth, I was disappointed with Jeb. It would have been fun to see the world with him. But if I was going to find Wonders, it

appeared I was going to find them alone. In Greece
or Africa or even Sassafras Springs.

"See you later?" asked Jeb.

"Yep," I said. "Come on, Sal," I told the dog. "Let's
go searching."

# Difficulties
# and Discoveries

Sal and I searched, but we didn't find much. On their farm up on the ridge, Piggy Ellis and his sisters stuck their tongues out at me when I asked about a Wonder. Their ma was canning beans and didn't have time to talk.

"Why ain't you home helping your pa?" she scolded. Like all the mowing and weeding and milking and feeding I'd been doing since five A.M. didn't count at all.

Next door at the Mayer place I got a friendlier welcome. I even got to sample Grandma Mayer's bread-and-butter pickles. They were tasty but not enough to amount to a Wonder.

The Culpepper place was below the Mayers', but I didn't spend much time there.

"You're Cole's crazy boy?" Ned Culpepper yelled as I approached. "Orville Payne told me to be on the lookout for you. He said I'd better bar the chicken-house door with you around."

I skedaddled out of there before I had a chance to ask him about Wonders or about his cousin Holt. At least I was learning when to keep my mouth shut.

I headed back to Yellow Dog Road. I had to get that sugar for my aunt, and maybe I'd have better luck in town. Halfway there, Sal doubled back, wagging her tail. I spun around to find out who she was so all-fired happy to see.

I wasn't happy to see that it was Rae Ellen Hubbell. "Hubbell" rhymes with "trouble."

"Are you following me?" I asked.

She stuck her nose up in the air. "It's a public road. Anybody can walk it."

"Well, you don't have to walk it so close to me."

"I was just about to say the same thing to you."

I looked down at Rae Ellen's dirty feet,

her yellow braids as straight as two pencils, her scrawny self drowning in a huge pair of overalls. My pals and I avoided Rae Ellen. We all knew she stole pie out of our lunch buckets at school.

"I thought you were looking for Wonderfuls," she said.

Leave it to Rae Ellen to get it all wrong. "Who told you that?"

"None of your business, but it was Maggie Austin."

I'd have to remind Jeb not to tell his sister my personal business again.

"Well, *I've* got a Wonderful," Rae Ellen announced.

This girl could give a fellow a pain in the neck. "Not Wonderfuls," I told her. "Wonders."

"I got one."

I knew there was no point talking to Rae Ellen, who didn't even have a lunch bucket of her own, much less a Wonder. She brought her lunch all rolled up in a blue bandanna that got limp and smelly by lunchtime.

"I'm busy now, Rae Ellen." I walked away, taking extra-big steps so she couldn't keep up with me. That didn't stop her from following me, so I tried to shut out the sound of her bare feet plopping along in the dust.

Closer to the general store, I saw Albert Bowie and his brother, Vern, walking toward me. They were carrying a heavy-looking barrel between them.

"What is that coming this way, Brother? Is it a circus parade?" asked Vern. He was older than Albert or Jeb or me—taller, stronger, and a lot more ornery. "Here comes a giraffe followed by a monkey."

I glanced behind me at Rae Ellen. "Are you still following me?".

"It's a free country," she answered.

I tried to ignore her. "What have you got in there?" I asked the Bowie brothers.

"Nails," said Albert. "Pa's gonna build a new hog pen."

The Bowies' hogs were the pride of the county, but I was glad we didn't live downwind of their farm.

Vern grinned. "So where are you and your girlfriend going?"

"Aw, you know Rae Ellen," I said. "She's a pest."

"I thought *he* was following *me*," said Rae Ellen.

"I'm going to the store for my mother." With that, she flicked her braids and walked around me, right past the Bowie brothers, down Yellow Dog Road, straight toward the general store.

Vern and Albert hooted at her, but she never looked back once.

Like I said, "Hubbell" rhymes with "trouble," and to my mind, Rae Ellen was anything but wonderful.

I would have liked to avoid the general store—and seeing Rae Ellen again—but there was that sugar and those clothespins I'd promised to get. So I ended up in town whether I wanted to go there or not. On one side of the street there was Yount's General—a combination general store and post office. Next door was Saylor's Feed and Supply Store, and next to that was the Rite-Time, a six-stool luncheonette run by Minnie Raymond. I would have liked a root beer along about then, but I didn't have a nickel to buy one.

Across from the stores was a row of houses where the Saylors, Miss Raymond, the Younts, and the preacher's family lived.

I didn't want to face Rae Ellen inside the store, so

I waited outside on the sagging bench near the gas pumps. Next to me on the wall was a faded notice that read HANDYMAN: CULLY PONE, RIDGE ROAD. NO JOB TOO BIG NOR SMALL.

No job at all, that's what Cully had. Just a doggone bookcase.

The screen door swung wide open with its usual squeal and out came Rae Ellen. She wasn't carrying anything.

"You still following me?" she asked.

This girl was plain annoying.

"I thought you had to get something for your ma."

Rae Ellen reached in her pocket and pulled out a spool of white thread. "So I did. What are you here for?"

"Trying to stay out of trouble, Hubbell."

She frowned and stalked off. I entered the store, leaving Sal napping in the shade of the bench.

As usual I wandered through the aisles, looking at all the things I wished I could buy. I fingered striped suspenders and stiff new overalls, peeked in the pickle barrel, and examined jars of peppermint sticks and jawbreakers.

Standing at the counter, talking to Hiram Yount,

was Violet Rowan. She handed over a huge basket brimming with fresh-picked herbs.

"You come by late tomorrow or the next day and I'll have your money," Mr. Yount told her.

Violet was the tallest and smartest girl in Sassafras Springs. Ever since her pa died, she was also the poorest. Mr. Rowan had been struck by lightning in his field a few years back. Word is, the lightning blew his boots right off his feet. They found them fifty yards from where he was lying.

Now Violet and her ma, Eulie, took in washing and sewing. Most folks couldn't afford to pay them to do their chores, so they also picked wild herbs from the hills. Goldenseal, horsetail, nettle, and red clover. A man from the city came into the store every few weeks and bought them to use in medicines.

In the winter the two of them made brooms to sell.

When Violet was fixing to leave, she spotted me over by the pickle barrel.

"Eben! Rae Ellen just told me you were looking for something wonderful!"

There were fireworks in Violet's bright blue eyes. "We've got just the thing you want!"

I pulled back because I thought she was going to grab me. I knew her from school, but us boys didn't spend much time around the older girls.

"Walk home with me and I'll show you," she said.

I was in a spot. Whatever Rae Ellen told her, it was probably wrong. And I didn't want to be seen walking with a girl, even a nice one like Violet. But her farm was right behind ours, so I couldn't pretend I had to go in another direction. Like I said, I was in a spot.

"Pa expects me home for the milking." I wasn't lying . . . entirely. "Maybe I could come tomorrow."

Some of the fire went out of Violet's eyes. "All right," she said. "But you will come tomorrow? Promise?"

"Sure," I said. "Cross my heart."

Once Violet was gone, Hiram's big voice boomed out across the store. "Well, Eben, what's this claptrap I hear about the Seven Wonders of the World?"

"Pa said he'd buy me a ticket to Colorado if I could find Seven Wonders here," I explained.

The storekeeper chuckled heartily. "I think your pa is pulling your leg. He knows you can't find seven folks to agree in Sassafras Springs, much less seven wonderful sights to see."

I must have looked disappointed, because Hiram leaned across the counter, as far as his big belly would allow him, and in a low voice said, "But your pa did send off a letter to Colorado yesterday. Just in case, I guess."

So Pa really believed I'd find Seven Wonders or he wouldn't have written Cousin Molly!

"Still, he's pretty safe making that offer." Hiram chuckled. "Now, what can I do for you?"

"Sugar," I told him. "And two packages of clothespins, please."

Ten pounds of sugar and two dozen clothespins felt like quite a load in that late afternoon heat, so I decided to travel cross-lots, which meant cutting across neighbors' farms. It kept me in the shade and out of the view of people going back and forth on the road. Especially Rae Ellen.

Sal thought it was a fine idea.

As I was passing the Community Church, the calm shade of the graveyard was mighty inviting. I knew the friends and neighbors residing there wouldn't pester me about Wonders—or anything else.

The summer air was so still and heavy you could practically grab it and hold it in your hand. It must have been ten degrees cooler in the churchyard, though. I set down the heavy sack, settled down under an old oak tree, and closed my eyes to think.

Finding Seven Wonders had sounded fine sitting on the porch. But now that Rae Ellen, Orville, and Hiram were involved, it seemed plain foolish. Still, there was the promise of a train, of a mountain, of an adventure that I couldn't get out of my head. My mind was drifting toward Colorado when suddenly Sal jumped up, whining.

"What is it, girl?" Sal's ears stood straight up. Then I heard a sound I'll never forget. It was like nothing I'd ever heard on this Earth before.

As I jumped up, I glimpsed the somber tombstones all around me. But the sound wasn't coming from the graveyard. It was coming from the church,

and it wasn't organ music either. The old organ had collapsed a few years back, so Mrs. Milton had to pound out hymns on an out-of-tune piano. But this wasn't piano music either.

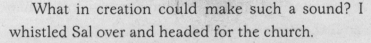

What in creation could make such a sound? I whistled Sal over and headed for the church.

It was cool and dark inside, and the strange music grew louder. I could make out the tune, but as many times as I've heard and sung the hymn, it never sounded like that before. The haunting notes didn't resemble an organ, a piano, a fiddle, or any instrument of this world. I half expected to find myself face-to-face with an angel playing a heavenly harp.

Somebody was sitting up near the pulpit. Even before my eyes got used to the darkness, I could see it was no angel. Angels never wore overalls and plaid shirts in the pictures I'd seen in Sunday school.

When I could see better, I recognized Calvin Smiley. I hadn't gotten to his place yet. He lived just outside Sassafras Springs in a cluster of small hardscrabble farms everybody called Bent Fork, because it was tucked in next to the bend of the creek. Pa told me once that folks down at Bent Fork didn't have much to work with, but they had high hopes. Though each farm there was no more than a shack and a square of land, Calvin's parcel mysteriously yielded more food per square inch than any other farm in the area.

Calvin's head was bent low over the instrument that was making that strange music. It wasn't a guitar or a fiddle, either, but he did have a bow in his hand.

Calvin looked up, startled. "Who's that?" he asked.

"It's me, Mr. Smiley. Eben McAllister. Cole McAllister's boy," I answered.

"Howdy, Eben. I was caught up in my practicing and didn't hear you come in," Mr. Smiley said. "Good to see you."

I finally made out what Calvin Smiley's instrument was, and I could hardly believe my eyes. In one of his coffee-brown hands was an ordinary handsaw, the kind used for cutting wood. In the other hand was a regular fiddler's bow.

"Were you playing *that*?" I asked.

"Heavenly days, young fellow. I've been playing this old saw since I was younger than you. Mrs. Milton had to go visit her sister in Leesville, so the preacher asked me to play my saw this Sunday," Mr. Smiley explained. "Thought I'd practice here in the church for a while. Would you like to give a listen?"

I slid into a pew as Calvin clamped the handle of the saw between his knees, with the saw teeth pointing toward him. With one hand, he held the flat tip of the saw and bent the blade off to the side, so it had a curve to it. Then he began to run the bow up and down across the dull edge of the saw, bending the blade back and forth as the sweet, sweet music started up again.

*Amazing Grace, how sweet the sound,*
*That saved a wretch like me.*

I had sung that tune a million times in church, but it had never sounded like this before. The music drifted across the pews, sweet and sad and hopeful all at once.

*I once was lost, but now am found,*
*Was blind, but now I see.*

The music hung in the air even after Mr. Smiley stopped playing. He put down his bow and stood up. "I think that'll satisfy the preacher, don't you, Eben?"

"Yes, sir," I answered. "I never heard anything like it. How'd you learn how to do that?"

"I saw a peddler play a saw once when I was just a pup, so I taught myself to play. Pop thought I was a fool at first," Calvin said. "Then came a day that changed his mind. Young man, no one ever laughed at my saw after that day. Pop thought this old saw was a positive marvel."

I perked up at the word "marvel." A marvel was like a Wonder. Could Mr. Smiley's musical saw be a genuine Wonder of Sassafras Springs?

"Like a Wonder of the World?" I asked eagerly.

"Eben, you'll have to decide that for yourself," said Calvin. "I don't know about the world. To me, what happened with this saw wasn't merely amazing. It was a miracle."

And if I got another Wonder when I wasn't even looking for one, that was a miracle of a kind too.

# Calvin Smiley's Story

### Amazing Grace

*We always called it the grasshopper summer. I was all of ten years old and it was one of the finest growing seasons Bent Fork had ever seen. The corn was tall and golden, and for once even poor folks like us felt like they might have cash in their pockets come fall.*

One morning my cousin Elroy came riding up like he'd seen his own ghost. He lived ten miles away and he'd worn his poor horse down. He was shouting so, it took us a spell to untangle what he was saying. We finally realized that a plague of locusts had eaten all his crops in two days flat, and they were headed toward our farm. Like it says in the Good Book, "they covered the face of the whole earth, so that the land was darkened; and they did eat every herb of the land, and all the fruit of the trees. . . ."

Those grasshoppers—that's what they were, in fact—had eaten everything green on Elroy's farm, including his wife's green dress that was hanging on the line!

We went right to work. Pop built fires all around the edges of our field, hoping the clouds of smoke would scare the grasshoppers away. Mama was afraid he'd burn up the good crops, but Pop said he'd burn 'em before he'd let the grasshoppers eat 'em.

It wasn't long till we heard 'em coming. To my dying day—which I hope is still some ways off—I will hear the buzzing of those millions of tiny wings. That sound made my skin crawl—still does, just to think of it.

The sky quickly took on that greenish color like it gets before a cyclone hits. A fast-moving cloud was sailing right toward us. Lord have mercy—this cloud was alive! A cloud of grasshoppers a mile across. The fires my pop set only seemed to attract 'em to us. Pop and Mama and my brothers and sisters and me all grabbed brooms and shovels and took to the fields and started swinging, vowing to beat 'em off if we had to.

Well, I swung and swung till my arm nearly fell off. After an hour those critters were still hungry. They could strip a cornstalk bare quick as you can snap your fingers. Pop tended the fires and Mama and us swung our brooms, but it was a losing battle. The noise of their buzzing got so loud, I could barely hear Mama and Pop yelling at us. I mostly saw their lips moving. Even after I covered my ears, I could still hear 'em. I thought I would lose my mind. I had to stop that sound.

Like a crazy person, I dropped my broom and ran for the barn. I could hear Pop yelling at me to come back there—the others yelled too. I didn't care. I grabbed my bow and started playing my old saw.

*'Twas grace, that taught my heart to fear,*
*And grace my fears relieved.*

It didn't bother me that Pop was furious. I'd have done anything to get that sound out of my ears. After a while, he was still yelling, but I couldn't believe what he was saying. "Bring that saw out here, boy— now. And keep on playing!"

I raced outside, sat on the rain barrel, and kept on playing. I closed my ears to those grasshoppers and I closed my eyes, too, and I played and played and played.

*How precious did that grace appear,*
*The hour I first believed.*

I felt my brother Ben shaking my shoulder. I opened my eyes and my ears, 'cause Ben was jumping up and down.

"Look, Cal, look! The grasshoppers are leaving!" he shouted. I could actually hear him again!

Sure enough, the waves of grasshoppers were retreating. Hallelujah! Although I'd never seen an ocean, I thought it looked like the tide going out. I heard my mama and pop shouting, "Keep playing, Cal! Keep playing!" So I played that old saw for all it was worth. And Mama and Pop and Ben and my sisters, Dolly and Dora, they all sang along.

*Through many dangers, toils, and snares,*
*I have already come.*
*'Tis grace hath brought me safe, thus far,*
*And grace will lead me home.*

They sang and I played until long after the cloud disappeared. Most all our crops were saved that summer. I didn't mind that the grasshoppers hated my music. All that mattered was that they left.

I was merely a humble instrument of the Lord that day. And the saw was my humble instrument. If you want to call anything a Wonder—glory be—this saw is a Wonder for certain.

"I will sing unto the Lord, because he hath dealt bountifully with me." Amen.

———

Calvin Smiley stared at his saw for a minute. "Amen," he repeated softly, sitting there with his head bowed.

"Mr. Smiley, do you still play that saw sitting out in your fields?" I was thinking of his rows of thriving crops. "Because maybe, the way things grow there . . ." I started to tell him my idea, but Calvin didn't let me finish.

"You're a smart boy, Eben," he said. "Yessir, a real smart boy."

He picked up his saw and went back to playing. The conversation was over.

I listened for a while, then quietly tiptoed back

outside with Sal at my heels. I leaned up against the oak, took out my tablet, and began to write about one more Wonder of Sassafras Springs as Calvin and his saw burst into the liveliest version of "Turkey in the Straw" ever heard in the graveyard of the Community Church.

## Day Four
# Smells and Spells

"Some folks in the city get Saturday afternoons off," Pa announced at breakfast without warning. "Maybe we ought to try that around Sassafras Springs."

"Are you sure you won't need me?" I was remembering what Jeb said about Pa selling the farm some day.

"What our corn needs isn't any more raking or weeding. It just needs time and a good soaking rain," said Pa.

I promised to work extra hard all morning. The next day was Sunday, and there would be no field work done.

The sun was blistering and there didn't seem to be enough water in the world to quench my thirst.

Pa rested with a bandanna over his face. For a second I thought he was shrinking in the blazing sun. Or maybe I was getting taller.

We raked till my arms ached. Pa told me aching arms were a good sign; they meant your muscles were growing. At the rate I was going, I'd be a match for the circus muscle man by evening.

Pa was true to his word that afternoon. But Sal and I had barely got started when I saw a skinny figure coming down the road.

"Hubbell Trouble," I whispered. "Let's get out of here."

We backtracked through the Austins' orchard toward the house. It was unusually quiet, and I wondered if the whole family had gone to visit Jeb's cousins. Jeb had irritated me some over the last few days, but I was disappointed to find the place was deserted. Even Dusty was gone.

I figured I'd head the back way down to Liberty Creek to cool off. On our way, Sal suddenly stopped and her ears perked up. I stopped too.

"Psst!"

As far as I could see, we were alone on the footpath that ran from the Austins' orchard to the meadow.

"Up here," a voice whispered. I looked up and saw a familiar face peering at me through the branches of a tree.

"What are you doing up there, Junior?" I asked. "Stealing peaches?"

"Who, me?" Junior Watkins dropped down from the branch so we were face-to-face. Or nose-to-forehead, as Junior was shorter and squarer than me.

Junior was the same age as Jeb and me. We weren't exactly bosom buddies, but since we were always lumped together in school and recess, we were friends of a sort.

"I heard you're looking for something." Junior was still whispering.

"Who said?"

"Everybody said." He acted like he was scared somebody was listening, even though there wasn't a soul around. "Well, I got something special."

"What is it?" I asked, full of doubt.

"If I tell you, will you keep it a secret?"

I was in a pickle. Whatever Wonders I found, I'd have to share with Pa or they wouldn't count. But I didn't want to pass up a possible Wonder either.

"Just tell me," I insisted.

"You won't tell my ma?"

"Promise." I could be truthful about that. Junior's ma was a powerful-looking woman, and I wasn't about to cross her.

"Come on!" Junior took off running across the meadow, and I tore off behind him with Sal at my heels. That dog never misses a thing.

I had no idea that Junior's stubby legs could move him so fast. We ran through more pastures and fields of beans until we got to his place. The Watkins family had a huge old gray barn and behind it, a tumbledown storage shack. Junior ran straight into the shed and I followed him.

When my eyes got used to the dark, I saw Junior reach into a jumble of junk and pull out an old wooden bucket covered with straw.

"You got to put them where it's hot, and this shed gets like a boiler," Junior explained as he plunged his hand into the bucket and ever so gently pulled out an egg.

"An egg? What kind of a Wonder is that?" I asked. "Everybody has eggs."

"Not like this." Junior looked so proud, I'd have thought he laid that egg himself. "I've got three of them."

"Well, eggs sure as shootin' aren't man-made, as any chicken would be happy to point out to you."

"It's not the eggs that are special. It's what I've done to them," Junior explained. "You know how we sometimes get an egg good and rotten so it makes a big stink?"

It was true, boys in Sassafras Springs had a custom of stealing an occasional egg, hiding it where their mothers wouldn't find it, aging it in the straw until it was good and rotten—oh, say a couple of weeks in hot weather. The hotter the better. When it was ready, they'd pick a time to let loose with it, creating a stench so great it would scare the stripes off a skunk.

"Everybody's done that," I told him.

"I know, but nobody's done it like me. Remember that rotten one I managed to shoot into the girls' outhouse at school last year?"

I could hardly forget that. It's the only time I know of when a rotten egg was launched by a slingshot. (Even Junior wasn't brave enough to go into the girls' outhouse.) The girls were shrieking and gagging at the smell, and Miss Collins let us off school early.

"But a Wonder is something important, Junior."

He held up the innocent-looking egg, gazing at it like it was a work of art. "Been here since May. Two hot months. Feel it."

I took the egg in my hand. The more rotten an egg gets, the lighter it gets, until it doesn't seem to weigh anything at all. I had to admit, this one was good and rotten.

"I got three of them. The rottenest eggs in Sassafras Springs." Junior sounded as if he'd just won the blue ribbon at the county fair.

"They're rotten, but they're not Wonders," I insisted. "Sorry, Junior. I've got to go."

"You'll think they're a Wonder when you smell them. And I'm not giving you any warning, either," Junior called after me. He sounded pretty mad.

Who'd have thought collecting a few Wonders would create such a big stink around Sassafras Springs?

That evening Aunt Pretty had supper all laid out on the porch when I got home.

"I can't stand that hot kitchen one more minute." She fanned herself with a dish towel. "We're eating a cold supper outside."

"Like a pic-a-nic," said Pa. He always added that extra "a" in picnic, and I liked the sound of it.

Aunt Pretty's cold supper was as tasty as most folks' hot meals. Cold chicken, cold cornbread, sliced tomatoes with thin slivers of onion on top, and her sour pickles. A glass of milk, cooled in the spring-house, for washing it down. A dish of cooked peaches left over from her day of preserving to top it off.

"What's the tally so far, Pretty?" asked Pa as he served himself a generous helping.

"Fifty-two jars," she answered. "Twenty jars of sliced peaches for pie, twenty-two jars of preserves for biscuits. Ten jars of spiced peaches. I'll do more tomorrow."

"It's enough to make a man long for winter." Pa turned to me. "What about you, son? Did you hit pay dirt?"

"Not today," I answered, realizing this was the first day I hadn't come up with a Wonder. "Ended up wasting my time."

Then I remembered the day before, down at the general store. I'd promised Violet I'd come by and see her Wonder. I still didn't believe she had one, but I had made a promise.

"I'm supposed to go to the Rowans', though."

Pa chuckled. "First place I'd go for a Wonder."

Aunt Pretty stood up, all business now. "Before you go, I'll pack up some chicken and peaches to take along."

"Do I have to?"

"Yes, you have to. The Rowans are having hard times, and they could use some building up. Now, Eulie's proud and she'll want to give you something in return. Just take whatever she offers."

Deep down, I was glad that, unlike other folks in Sassafras Springs, Aunt Pretty didn't mind her own business, at least when her neighbors had problems. Before long, I was lugging a basket of food across our field to the Rowans' small spread, which backed onto ours.

"Eben, you came!" Violet called out.

Long shadows promised it would be dark before long, but Eulie and Violet were still working outside.

"Howdy, Eben." Eulie leaned back on the heels of the huge black shoes she always wore in the garden. They were the same work boots Violet wore to get to school in the snow last winter. Every time I saw them, I couldn't help wondering if they were the ones that blew off Mr. Rowan's feet when the lightning struck.

"Aunt Pretty sent this," I said, handing over the basket.

"Goodness, she is a generous one," said Eulie, peeking inside at all the goodies.

Violet wasn't interested in goodies. "Tell her, Eben. About the Wonders. Rae Ellen called them 'Wonderfuls,' but I knew you meant Wonders. Like the Great Pyramid and the Hanging Gardens."

I told you Violet was smart.

I cleared my throat and faced Eulie. "Ma'am, I'm trying to find Seven Wonders here in Sassafras Springs. Like a pyramid. Or a giant lighthouse."

"Thank goodness there are no pyramids around here," laughed Eulie. "Seems I heard about some kind of a curse on that one they found last year."

Violet jumped up. "You have something special, Ma! Show him."

Eulie looked doubtful. "It doesn't resemble a pyramid in the least."

"Show him, Ma. He'll like it. I'll finish the weeding." I haven't seen Violet that excited since she won the spelling bee.

"Well, all right! Come along." Eulie started toward the door, beckoning for me to follow. Sal was content to stay outside with Violet.

"Now don't expect anything fancy," Eulie warned me.

Believe me, it was hard to imagine anything fancy in their shabby cottage.

She led me to her small kitchen table, its edges worn smooth by generations of soap and water. It looked like any table in Sassafras Springs. That and two chairs were about all the decoration in the place. A blanket hung from the ceiling, and I could see the shadow of a bed behind it. In the middle of the table was a single oil lamp.

"This is it," said Eulie, stroking the wood like it was her favorite cat. "Not a Wonder, maybe, but special. Because *this* is the table that walked through a graveyard. Walked on its own, or so folks would tell you."

She had my attention then. "What's that, ma'am?" I asked, fishing my pencil out of my pocket.

"Sit yourself down and I'll tell you," said Eulie. "I'll tell you the absolute truth."

# Eulie Rowan's Story

---

## The Four-Legged Haint

*Sassafras Springs used to be even quieter than it is now. When the moon was a sliver, it was dark as a pocket outside. Not many lights, not many people. It was a lonely place.*

Folks had more time to gossip, too. It didn't take long for word to spread that there was a "haint" in the graveyard. A haint is what the old-timers called a ghost.

This was no ordinary ghost. And there have been other ghosts in Sassafras Springs. Why, for years after old Mrs. Gardner died, she'd show up in church on Christmas Eve. No one would go near that pew. And there was the golden ghost of Liberty Woods. But that's not the ghost I'm telling you about. This was a table folks saw—yes, a table walking through the tombstones, night after night, according to some. Not only did it give off a strange light, this table made an eerie wailing sound, like no human ever made. That's what folks said, anyway.

When word spread, nobody would go in the graveyard at night. Folks started locking their doors at night for the first time. Most people were superstitious around Sassafras Springs. Most still are. Maybe I'm one of them.

There was one person around who wasn't superstitious. However, she was plenty suspicious. She thought the idea of a table walking was plain silly. Even though a table does have legs.

Her name was Rose-Ivy, and she was a flame-haired beauty who lived alone up on Osage Hill. Her mama and papa had died when she was eighteen, and she stayed on the farm, keeping a few animals, selling herbs like Violet and I do. Most folks thought she couldn't make it on her own, that she should sell the place and go live with relatives. *Most folks should mind their own business,* Rose-Ivy thought. Besides, she didn't give up easily. Deep down she thought maybe that was why she'd survived the illness that took her parents.

Since Rose-Ivy took everything she heard with a grain of salt, she didn't think the story about the haint made sense. Why would a ghost look like a table? How could a table make a wailing noise?

One night when there was a full moon to guide her, she took her lantern and set out for the graveyard. She didn't have a gun or a knife, just her old pointer dog by her side. If there was a ghost—which she knew there wasn't—a gun wouldn't do much good. If there was a ghost—which common sense told her there wasn't—a good pair of legs could probably outrun it.

The first thing Rose-Ivy saw when she got there was a light moving between the markers. She and her dog stopped and watched. There she saw it, plain as day, a four-legged table walking along with the light, weaving in and out among the tombstones. It was quite a sight. Rose-Ivy stayed still and watched. Suddenly the light stopped. So did the table. Rose-Ivy's dog whined and she shushed him. She blew out her lantern so the haint wouldn't see her.

She stood stock-still in the moonlight until she heard the yowling. The dog tried to run but Rose-Ivy

held him back. The sound was truly like the howl of a ghost, the kind that gets inside you and it chills your bones. Rose-Ivy didn't move a muscle or even a hair as she listened.

Finally the wailing stopped and a human voice cried out, "Mary! Why did you leave me, Mary?"

That set Rose-Ivy in motion. Instead of running away, she inched closer to the table. Her dog followed, tail between his legs. When she got closer she took a good look at the table sitting among the graves. A lantern on the table gave off enough light to see that it was set with a plate, and a knife and fork, and a basket of food. There was a chair next to the table. And someone was sitting on that chair. Someone too solid to be a ghost.

It was a man, and he was sobbing his heart out, calling, "Mary, how could you leave me? Why didn't you take me with you?" Rose-Ivy realized that the table was next to the tombstone of a young woman who had died three months before. That woman's name was Mary.

"Is that you, Tom?" Rose-Ivy asked the sobbing man. It was his turn to be startled. It was Thomas Fitzgerald, the husband of the woman who'd died.

Rose-Ivy moved in closer. "What are you doing out here in the pitch-dark?"

The man moaned. "Lord, I miss her so much. I can't stand to eat alone in the house without my Mary. So I come out here every night to be with her," Tom told her, the tears glistening on his cheeks.

"Tom Fitzgerald, you're going to get yourself shot, creeping around in graveyards at night. You've been scaring folks half to death! You come home now and eat supper with me. I don't like to eat alone either," said Rose-Ivy. "Come along right now."

She sounded determined, and Tom was so surprised that he actually said yes. He left his table and chair by Mary's tombstone and went up Osage Hill with Rose-Ivy. They had a good supper and a good strong cup of coffee, and when the meal was over, Rose-Ivy told him to come back for dinner the next night too.

The next day Tom took his table and chair back home. He went to Rose-Ivy's house for dinner that night and the next night and the night after that. He talked about his dear Mary, and Rose-Ivy talked about her departed family, and sometimes Tom brought her some beans or corn from his garden or a bunch of wildflowers. And sometimes Rose-Ivy sent back some food for Tom's lunch the next day.

Folks talked for a while, until they found other things to gossip about. And they stopped locking their doors at night.

At the end of a year Tom married Rose-Ivy, and they raised a family of their own. But every day, winter and summer for the rest of her life, Rose-Ivy visited Mary's grave, planting flowers, tending to the weeds, and talking to her, so she knew she wasn't forgotten.

And that's the true story of this very table, the table that walked in the graveyard.

---

Eulie thumped the table loudly with both hands, which made me jump. When I recovered, I asked her, "Was that the graveyard at the Community Church?"

"The same."

That gave me pause. I'd just been sitting there among the tombstones the day before.

"How'd you end up with the table?"

"Son, I've been sitting at this table since I was a baby. Don't you know my parents' names?" she asked.

I shook my head. "No, ma'am."

"Thomas and Rose-Ivy Fitzgerald," she stated proudly. "I still put flowers on Mary Fitzgerald's grave to this day. And I expect Violet will do the same after I'm gone. Violet's got her grandma's fiery hair—and her fiery spirit too, I hope."

"Then it's all true?"

"True as anything I know. Will that help you, Eben?" asked Eulie.

"Yes, ma'am." I began to scribble on my pad. I kept writing, right out the door.

"It was a Wonder, wasn't it, Eben?" It was almost dark, but Violet was still kneeling alongside the peppers and lettuce. She looked different now. Even in her shapeless dress, even with dirty hands and feet, she looked positively rich as she handed me Aunt Pretty's basket, which she'd filled with lettuce, onions, and cucumbers.

"A positive Wonder," I told her, and I meant it.

But I'm telling you, I was grateful that I didn't have to pass through the graveyard on the way home.

Later that night I went to sleep just fine. Then I had this dream where I was walking in the graveyard alone, without even Sal by my side, and I saw a glowing thing passing between the tombstones. I could tell it was no table because it walked upright like a man.

I called out, "Who is that?" and the shining thing swiveled around. It was a man in his long johns and he didn't have a face.

I sat up in bed, wide awake and shaking, and I had no interest in going back to sleep.

I got up and leaned out the front window to fill my lungs with fresh, cool air. The sight of the moonlit barn, the shadowy oak, and the outline of Redhead Hill was a comfort. I noticed a light flickering below me. When I leaned farther out, I saw Aunt Pretty sitting on the front porch in her big white nightgown.

I'd never seen my aunt so quiet, just sitting and staring out at the farm.

Was she thinking about what happened to Holt Nickerson and why he never came back? Was she wondering if he was still out there, riding that horse in his long johns?

I'll never know, because that's the kind of question a boy doesn't ask his maiden aunt.

Day Five
# Into the Woods

Whatever happened the night before, Aunt Pretty
was chipper the next morning as we made our way
down to church. I half expected to see a faceless fellow wearing long johns or a table all laid out for dinner as we passed through the graveyard, but all I saw
were butterflies flitting around the tombstones,
especially the one with the purple and pink flowers
all around it. I squinted my eyes. MARY HAYNES
FITZGERALD, the marker read. I should have known
it. Some of the flowers were violets.

During the service, when Calvin played "Amazing
Grace," I could hear that cloud of bugs buzzing
toward Sassafras Springs. In Sunday school I tried
hard not to see Miss Zeldy in my mind. I decided to

try picturing myself in Colorado, so when Mrs. Pritchard asked me how big a mustard seed was, she caught me off guard. "High as a mountain," I answered. She was surprised, but she said that was the general idea—that it grew big because of faith.

Later folks congregated outside to chat. Since they didn't work in their fields and gardens on the Sabbath, our neighbors weren't in a big hurry to go home. Neither was Aunt Pretty. I was itching to get our big Sunday dinner over with so I could round up a couple more Wonders. After all, there'd be no chores until evening. With a whole day before me, I might be able to finish my entire list.

My aunt was too busy chitchatting with the other ladies to think about dinner. Pa was in the middle of a long conversation with Marvin Peevey, the mayor of Sassafras Springs. Suddenly Reverend Carson grabbed hold of me. (Folks liked to call him Parson Carson, but only behind his back.)

"What's this I hear about you looking for Wonders?" he asked in his booming preacher's voice.

"It's kind of a game," I explained.

"Stick to the Good Book, Eben. You'll find all the signs and wonders you'll ever need there."

"Yes, sir," I answered. "That's good advice."

I didn't have the nerve to suggest he preach on the theme of "love thy neighbor," but some members of his congregation, like Orville Payne, could stand to hear it.

Somebody else grabbed Parson Carson's attention, and I went looking for Jeb. I found him under the big maple tree, trying to keep his brothers and sisters from getting dirty. It was not an easy job.

"I stopped by yesterday but nobody was home," I told him.

"Had to go see my cousins," he said.

"I figured."

"Got a plan for after Sunday dinner," said Jeb. "We'll go dig worms and sell them for bait on Monday so's we can buy ourselves a root beer at the Rite-Time."

"I want root beer," Flo whined.

"Sounds tempting, but I've got something else to do," I told him.

"I know, the Wonders." Jeb sounded disappointed. "Maybe we can find one down at the creek."

"Maybe," I said, but I didn't believe it. Still, looking for Wonders could be a little lonely, even with

Sal along. "If we can ever get dinner over, I can look around some and still make it to the creek."

I glanced over at Aunt Pretty, but she showed no sign of moving on. I decided to see if I could hurry her up.

She was talking to Lessie Mull when I approached.

"I've got a hankering for your good fried chicken," I told my aunt. Flattery never hurts with her, as long as it's based on truth.

Mrs. Mull poked her pointy face out from under the brim of her yellow sunbonnet. "Eben, I hear tell you've been paying visits around Sassafras Springs."

"Just asking folks if they have something special to show me."

"Mrs. Payne says Orville caught you snooping around. Of course, I'm sure you meant no harm."

Aunt Pretty snorted. "Poor Almeta. Orville has plenty to hide, if you get my meaning." She brought a cupped hand to her mouth in a gesture that meant one thing: drinking. That habit was frowned on by both the Baptist and the Community Churches, except for medicinal purposes.

"I have nothing to hide," said Lessie. "Eben, if you want to see something special, come over and I'll show you my log cabin quilt. I was just a young woman when I won second place at the county fair with that quilt."

"Yes, ma'am," I answered, even though everybody had a log cabin quilt somewhere. Aunt Pretty had two or three.

"Well, Lessie, this boy looks hungry," Aunt Pretty said at last. "I guess I'll have to feed him."

As we left the churchyard, Lessie called after me, "You come on over and see it, boy."

After Aunt Pretty's big Sunday spread, Sal and I trudged back up Yellow Dog Road. Though my full stomach slowed me down a bit, I was feeling hopeful . . . until I heard footsteps running down the hill behind me. Without a doubt, Rae Ellen Hubbell knew how to ruin a perfectly nice afternoon.

"Are you ready for my Wonderful now?"

"No, I am not." I took a firm tone with Rae Ellen.

"Well, Junior Watkins's Wonderful didn't pan out, did it?"

Sassafras Springs didn't have a newspaper, and we didn't need one either with Rae Ellen poking her nose into everybody's business.

"I may have to call the county sheriff and tell him you're making a nuisance of yourself," I told her.

"Ha, ha, ha." Rae Ellen didn't sound the least bit scared. "You don't have an idea of where to look, and I have a Wonderful for you. So you might as well see it."

"I'm looking for *Wonders*. And I'm looking alone."

I set off down the road at a fast clip. I knew she was behind me, but I didn't look back, not all the way down to town.

On Sunday, what few businesses we had in Sassafras Springs were closed. Hiram used to keep the gas pumps open, but there wasn't enough traffic to make it worth his while.

Sal and I crossed the County Road and headed for the creek. Jeb was already there, fishing.

"I thought you were looking for Wonders," he said.

"I thought you were going to dig worms."

Jeb grinned. "Already did. I got a full bucket, so I decided to do some fishing."

I squatted down next to him. "Better not let Parson Carson see you."

"The fish must know it's Sunday," said Jeb. "I haven't had a nibble. At least I don't have to look after the young'uns."

Jeb's parents always gave Maggie and him Sunday afternoon off.

"Gee whiz, it's boiling hot!" I lay back flat on the rock with my feet dangling in the cool creek water. "I'm trying to ditch Rae Ellen," I explained, taking a quick look behind me. She was nowhere to be seen.

But Maggie and another girl from school, Carrie, were wading through the water toward us. Maggie was scrawny as a stick, but us boys admired her because she was the only girl ever to win the watermelon-seed-spitting contest at the Sunday School Picnic. Carrie was teacher's pet, but she deserved to be, since she never did a bad thing in her life.

"Coogie Jackson's got a Wonder for you!" said Maggie, waving her arms toward the woods. "He wants you to come—now."

Coogie (short for Jacob Coogan) Jackson had a Wonder? Now that got my attention. Coogie was no ordinary boy. At six, he ate a fly on a nickel bet and declared it tasted fine. At eight, he kissed a toad in exchange for a dish of ice cream. He said it tasted like chocolate (the toad and the ice cream both).

At nine, Coogie ate a June bug on a dare. He rubbed his belly and said June bugs had more flavor and crunch than flies. He liked them both fine.

Last year Coogie Jackson ate some leaves for two bits and got poison ivy all through his throat and innards. They thought he'd die, but he managed to pull through . . . barely. He ended up a little thinner, a little paler, and a lot hoarser than before.

Some of us would try to rile him about it. "Got a tickle in your throat, Coogie?" we'd ask. Or "Eat any good leaves lately?"

Coogie never got upset, but he didn't eat anything for money after that either. Still, he had our respect. He knew things the rest of us would never know. That gave him power.

I sat up straight. "Is it true, Carrie?" I asked, knowing she wouldn't ruin her reputation by lying.

Carrie nodded. "He told me himself. Come on, I'll show you."

It was hard to pass up a summons from Coogie, and it was hard to pass up a Wonder, except if it was from Rae Ellen.

Jeb and I got up to follow the girls. Sal was already way ahead of the rest of us.

There was nothing like a bridge over Liberty Creek, but there were spots where you could walk across a trail of fallen trees and big rocks to get to the other side. We followed the girls deep into the woods, to a place I'd never been. Jeb and I'd tried to explore those woods a few times, but if the chiggers didn't discourage us, the poison ivy did. I wasn't happy about going over there, but like I said, Coogie had power.

We stopped in a small clearing, in front of an old, abandoned outhouse, weathered to the color of ashes and looking like a gust of wind would knock it flat. There were inch-wide gaps in the splintering wood and a tangle of weeds wrapped around it.

There was nothing unusual about an outhouse in Sassafras Springs. Most folks still thought a bathroom inside the house was unnecessary, expensive, maybe even unsanitary, though Aunt Pretty sighed a lot when she read about big-city houses with indoor plumbing and wringer washers and iceboxes.

This outhouse hadn't been used in a long, long time. What it was doing out in the middle of nowhere was a puzzle. There was no house or even a shack in those woods. And you sure as shooting don't need an out-house if you don't have folks living nearby.

Deep in the woods, you don't need a bathroom at all.

"Are you funning me?" I asked, trying to make my voice low and even, like Pa's.

Coogie stepped out from behind the back of the

outhouse. He had hair the color of cotton. If he wasn't a boy, you'd have thought he was a white-haired old man. Instead, he was a white-haired young man, with pale skin and light blue eyes and almost-white lashes.

Albert Bowie stepped out from behind him, like he was Coogie's shadow.

"What took you so long?" Coogie asked in his husky voice.

"I hope you're not telling me this old outhouse is a Wonder," I told him. "Looks more like a calamity."

"You want a Wonder or not? I might decide to go home if you're not interested."

"You'd better listen," said Albert. "He's got a humdinger for you."

I bit my tongue to keep from saying, "Who doesn't?"

"I want to hear it," said Maggie, almost breathless.

"Me too," said Carrie.

Nobody on Earth, except maybe Pa, could have kept me from hearing that story, but I didn't want Coogie to know it.

"I only have a few minutes," I warned him.

"Good enough," said Coogie. He pointed to a fallen tree nearby. "Have a seat and I'll tell you why this outhouse is a Wonder of the World."

Maggie, Carrie, and Jeb plopped down as they were told, but not me. I stood face-to-face with Coogie.

"How would you know?" I asked. As much as I wanted a Wonder, I was suspicious.

"My pa told me. Maybe you don't know it, but he didn't come from around here. He come all the way from Gladiola, Georgia."

"So what?" I asked. After all, my pa's people came to Sassafras Springs by way of Virginia. Every family started somewhere else, except maybe the Indians.

"It's not where he come from that's important," said Coogie. "It's how he come here. Do you want this dang Wonder or not?"

It sounded like a challenge.

"I'm listening," I told him. But I still didn't sit down.

# Coogie Jackson's Story

## Flight from Georgia

*It's my pa's story, but he don't tell it often 'cause he figures no one would believe him. The truth is hard to swallow sometimes. Anyway, Gladiola is a good five hundred miles from Sassafras Springs as the crow flies. Pa says even a crow couldn't get from there to here in ten minutes. That's exactly how long it took my pa to get here. They was the longest ten minutes of his life.*

He come in this very outhouse. It may not look like much now, but it was the finest outhouse made by man. My grandpappy built it with his own two hands. Pa told me my grandpappy said the devil himself couldn't knock this one over.

See, there was a bunch of scalawags around

Gladiola—family by the name of Pitt. They gave Pa a terrible time at school. Gave everybody a terrible time. They scared the little girls and cheated at games and even tried to burn the school down. They ran roughshod over the whole county—tearing down fences so the cows would get loose, helping themselves to everybody's crops, and stealing the storekeeper blind.

But their favorite trick of all was knocking over outhouses. You might say it was a hobby of theirs. They'd let a person get good and settled inside, then rush up and tip it over. It'd take a while for the victim to crawl out, but the yelling started right away.

They did it to Grandpappy late one night, and he was madder than anything. He vowed that would never happen to him again, and he set to building a tip-proof outhouse! My pa says everybody thought he'd lost his mind. He let the crops go to seed and hammered on the dang thing night and day. He had a few failures and had to start over, but Pa says he was busting with pride when he finished.

It was a two-seater with a window, so if there was mischief, Grandpappy could look out and see who the culprits were.

He made Pa and his brother try and tip it over. "Harder! Push harder," he yelled at them. Well, Pa was sixteen and pretty strong, but that old outhouse wouldn't budge. Grandpappy said it was solid as the rock of ages.

I don't know if those Pitts ever tried to tip it over, but if they did, they must have been disappointed. Anyway, Grandpappy and his family could sit in that outhouse with no worry of being tipped again!

Then there come a scorcher of a day in August. The air got heavy and still. The sky had a sickly greenish color. And whoever heard of a green sky?

Pa felt the call of nature and ducked inside the outhouse.

He wasn't setting there long when he heard what sounded like a train coming—and it sounded like it was coming right for the outhouse. However, the train didn't even pass near their farm, much less Gladiola. As he was pondering that thought, the outhouse started bumping and bouncing like a bucking bronco. He figured the Pitt family was back again. He held on tight to the seat and waited for the outhouse to tip over, but the banging and the shaking got worse.

Just as Pa thought Judgment Day had come, the outhouse started spinning around like the merry-go-round at the county fair.

He decided to look out the window and see how the Pitts could manage this. Was he surprised to see he was surrounded by fluffy white clouds! He wasn't on the ground no more—he was flying high, smack dab in the middle of a cyclone!

He thought he was on his way to heaven, and he hoped he'd be able to stay there. So any little bad thing he ever done—a white lie here, a small mistake there—whirled through his mind as he twirled through the clouds.

Next, a funny thing happened. The clouds parted and Pa could look out the window and see what was under him. What he saw was pure amazing: blue water as far as the eye could see. It was the ocean, rolling right under him! Quick as a blink, he was looking down on castles. He must have been going over Spain or England. He spun around some more and saw those mountains with the snow on top. The Alpines. Before he knew it, he was over that Big Wall of China, right next to the famous Pyramids of India!

He rubbed his eyes, thinking he was dreaming,

and when he looked down, he was over a big old desert somewhere and whoosh—he was gazing down at blue waters again. He spun around faster and faster and higher and higher, and you know what? He was whirling over ice and snow in all directions. There was the North Pole, with Santy Claus waving at him!

Pa didn't have a chance to wave back, 'cause he twirled his way straight down along a big river that was so muddy, it had to be the Mississipp. He held on for dear life as the outhouse started jerking and jolting, 'most shaking his teeth loose. Pa figured this was the end, and while he was preparing himself, the outhouse dropped straight down and hit the ground like a load of bricks.

Pa says it got real still, real quiet. Quiet as snow falling. Quiet as, well, dead quiet. It took a while for him to get up the courage to look out the window. He dang sure didn't know what to expect. But he took a deep breath and looked out and saw: this. He had landed on this actual spot. All the way from Gladiola, Georgia, clear across the world, to Sassafras Springs by way of one of the biggest, baddest cyclones to hit the country!

He was stunned at first. Shucks, who wouldn't be? He wandered outside, kind of ginger-like. He stumbled his way across the creek, to the General. Hiram Yount's father run it back then. He called the preacher, who listened to the story and let my pa stay at his place for a while. Pa wrote home and got a letter back saying that the cyclone had flattened the house, killing my grandpappy. Grandma and the other young'uns were all right, but they'd lost everything. Poor Grandpappy Jackson. If he'd built his house like he built his outhouse, he might still be alive today.

And that's the story of this here Wonder: The outhouse that flew around the world.

———

I looked over at Jeb, Maggie, and Carrie. Their jaws were just about setting on the ground. I guess mine was too. I never heard such a story before.

Albert stepped forward. "You putting that down with your Wonders?" he asked.

"You got any proof?"

Albert and Coogie exchanged a quick look. "I got proof," said Coogie. "You go inside there. You'll see those two seats, and next to the window, my pa scribbled a map of what he saw. Dated and signed it, right there on the wall."

My good sense made me hesitate.

"There's your proof, waiting," said Albert, pointing at the door. "Go on."

So I went inside and the door slammed hard behind me. Right away I noticed something wrong: There was one seat, not two. I turned to the window, looking for some writing and a map. I realized I'd been had about one second before that rickety, rackety, falling-down outhouse tipped on its side.

I crashed down with it and lay there, listening to Coogie and Albert whooping and hollering outside, and Jeb and the girls giggling up a storm.

I'd been had and I should have known better. I was probably the only person in Sassafras Springs, except for Violet Rowan, who knew the Great Pyramid was in Egypt, not India like he'd said.

And that thing about Santy Claus waving, well, like I said, I'd been had.

I crawled over to the window, which was way down low to the ground.

"Go eat some leaves, Coogie Jackson!" I shouted. "Go eat poison ivy!"

He kept on laughing and I didn't blame him.

Sal came up to the window, sniffing and whining, but I was in no hurry to get up. I stayed in there, thinking, until the light coming in through the window started to fade.

"You can come out now. They're gone," I finally heard Jeb say.

I crawled out through the window.

"That Coogie," I grumbled, brushing spider webs off my clothes.

"Sorry you got tricked," said Jeb. "It was a good whopper, though, don't you think?"

"Yep. But it wasn't a Wonder."

Jeb snickered. "That thing about Santy Claus, that was good."

I shook my head. "Coogie Jackson would do or say anything."

On my way home, I wondered how long it would take

me to live the whole thing down. The girls had already told Rae Ellen, no doubt, and Albert wouldn't be shy about spreading the word. I was ready to hop a train to Colorado and never come back.

Pa was heading out of the barn when I got back home.

"Find yourself a Wonder?" he asked.

"Naw. Just saw some friends down at the creek. Pa, you know about an old outhouse in the woods?"

"Other side of the creek?"

I nodded.

"Built by a fellow, oh, twenty years ago," said Pa. "He was a squatter who pitched a tent in the woods and built that outhouse."

Pa stared out at the barn with a faraway look in his eyes.

"He seemed like a nice enough fellow until Marvin Peevey found out he was stealing folks' horses and selling 'em over in Oak Grove. The fellow picked up his tent and left in a hurry, but he had to leave his outhouse behind. I can't believe it's still standing."

"It's not, after today."

Pa looked over at me, squinting his eyes. "You in some kind of trouble?"

"No. I was tricked and tricked good by Coogie Jackson. And I'm never going to live it down," I said.

"Folks forget over time," Pa said after a long pause. "I know some upstanding people who've lived down worse than that. I'm not going to tell you which ones, though."

When we got to the porch, Aunt Pretty was sitting in her rocker, but for once, instead of crocheting, she was sewing with a needle and thread, and she wasn't darning socks, either.

"What's that you're making?" Pa asked.

"Well, a boy can't travel on a train in rags and tatters, can he? I'm making Eben a new shirt. And I'm going to take Grandpa's old trousers out of the trunk in the attic and cut them down too."

"Going to knit him up some shoes, too?" Pa asked with a twinkle in his eyes.

Aunt Pretty chuckled. "Could if I had a mind to do it."

I was feeling confused. "Aunt Pretty, I thought you didn't approve of me going."

"At first I was vexed, I admit. Sometimes folks go

away and don't come back. But I'm pleased for you to take a trip, Eben. I just have my concerns. You seem to have forgotten, Cole, that no one was too happy when Molly married Eli—him being a complete stranger she'd known for about a week."

"That was twenty years ago." Pa slapped at a mosquito. "Guess he's no stranger to Molly anymore."

Aunt Pretty's needle darted in and out of the white cloth. "Don't even know where those two live," she muttered. "Might live in a tent for all we know."

"A tent would be nice and cool in summer." Pa gave me a wink. "Yessir, I might try that sometime."

A slight smile played across Aunt Pretty's lips. "Maybe I'd better knit Eben a nice warm sweater, just in case."

The conversation was getting under my skin. "I haven't got seven Wonders yet." I glanced at Pa. "I just wasted a whole afternoon on a joke."

"Goodness gracious, you have two whole days left," said Aunt Pretty. "Now stand up, let me see if this will fit."

She held the cloth up against my shoulders and said it'd fit just fine, but I had a strong suspicion I wasn't going anywhere. It was the first day I hadn't actually gotten a Wonder, and I was feeling gun-shy about showing myself in public again.

I sat down on the front step, feeling downright sorry for myself. What good on Earth were four Wonders? I might as well have gone fishing for four days.

Aunt Pretty put down her sewing and excused herself to put supper on the table. She stopped at the door and sniffed the air. "Smells like rain coming."

"High time," said Pa.

After a while the yard took on that purply look it gets after the sun has hit the horizon. Pa stretched and sighed and I could tell he was getting ready to go out and do the milking, so I jumped up first and grabbed a lantern.

"Let me, Pa. I can handle it by myself."

Pa looked surprised but pleased. I was pleased too, since Myrt and Mabel were probably the only two females in Sassafras Springs that hadn't heard about the outhouse yet.

I was relaxing to the steady splashing of the milk hitting the pail when I heard a rustling noise. Myrt looked nervous, and Sal jumped up and ran to the barn door.

Standing in the doorway was trouble herself: Rae Ellen Hubbell, carrying a raggedy old burlap bag.

"What are you doing here?" My tone of voice made it clear I wasn't happy to see her.

"You need another Wonderful, so I figured, if you're not going to come to me, I'll bring it to you." She raised the burlap sack so I could see it.

I sighed. "Rae Ellen, I'm milking here."

She perched herself on a hay bale and said, "I can wait."

Wait she did, for Myrt was not a cow to be hurried and neither was Mabel.

Just about the time I was finished, Pa came out to take the milk buckets. He didn't seem surprised to see Rae Ellen there. He just said, "Howdy," and told me he'd have Aunt Pretty hold my supper for me while I entertained my guest.

I was about to say that guests were folks you actually invited, but I knew he'd get on me for being rude.

Once he was gone, Rae Ellen slid off the hay bale and brought her sack over to me. "Do you want to see my Wonderful or not?"

"It better be good," I warned her.

Rae Ellen led me to the window, carefully opened the bag, and reached inside.

"It's a ship in a bottle." Rae Ellen's voice quivered. "My uncle Dutch gave it to me."

I stared at the dusty bottle. The tiny ship inside didn't impress me much. "I know how they do it," I bragged. "They collapse the boat, stick it in the bottle, and pull it up again with a string. It's a trick, not a Wonder."

"Eben McAllister, are you dumb as a post? This isn't some regular old ship in a bottle. This is a real live ship with a cargo of pure and terrible evil!" Rae Ellen's eyes widened as she paused. "Now, are you going to write this down or not?"

"Aw, go on," I said, pulling out my tablet. "But make it fast."

## Rae Ellen's Story
———•—•———
## Dark Seas

*Uncle Dutch says in summer he'd watch the waves of corn out in the field and all he could think about was the ocean and cool water and tropical breezes. As soon as he was old enough, he snuck out of the house and went east, looking for the sea and a job on a ship.*

He didn't know diddly about ships or sailing, so he had to tell a big fib to get a job as a cabin boy. He went on a great big ship, the S.S. *Phantom of the Sea.* A phantom is a ghost, you know. Anyway, the ship was heading for Africa. That's about as far away as you can go.

Uncle Dutch says back in the cornfields he hadn't thought about seasickness and bad food and nasty sailors, and that's what he found there. But he liked the blue waves and the cool breezes, and his belly got used to the ship rocking after a while.

The big problem was the captain of the ship. His name was Captain Graves, and he was meaner than Old Lady Ellis. She won't even let me take a shortcut through her orchard. Says I stole apples! Anyway, the captain, he kept all the good food and drink locked up for himself while the crew half starved. He treated the sailors like dirt—worse than dirt, worse than you boys treat us girls. Uncle Dutch says he was skin and bones after a few weeks, and the whole crew was grumbling about Captain Graves.

Well, they reached the tip of Africa, and they were supposed to go all the way around the Cape of something-or-other. Then the most awfullest, terrible storm hit the S.S. *Phantom of the Sea*. The sailors were scared out of their wits, especially Uncle Dutch! The waves whooshed over the deck. Lightning struck all around them. Finally, the first mate—he's the head sailor—knocked on the captain's door.

Captain Graves was mad as all get-out that somebody disturbed him 'cause he'd been drinking his expensive "likker" from France or some such place.

The first mate told him the crew was scared and wanted to sail into a safe harbor for the night. They knew they were close to land. That mean captain cussed him with bad words, Eben—real bad, so bad I can't say them.

"I am afraid of nothing on heaven or Earth," he said, and he slammed the door in the first mate's face. Bang!

Uncle Dutch says he prayed for the storm to let up, but it got worse and worser. He hung on to the side of the ship for dear life, and all he could think about were the rows of corn waving in the hot sun. He swore if he ever got to land safely, he'd never set foot on a ship again.

That's what he was thinking when a huge wave crashed against the deck and washed two sailors overboard right before his eyes. The crew sent down whatchamacallits—life peaservers—to fish them out, but no one ever laid eyes on them again. The rest of the crew was wailing like ghosts, which Uncle Dutch says he thought they were soon going to be.

So they went back to the captain's cabin and the first mate knocked.

This time the captain was roaring mad when he

opened the door. His eyes were bloodshot and his breath was hot.

"Bunch of quivering cowards" he called them and said that all of them together didn't have the courage of one real man like him. "God will not sink my ship—he wouldn't dare!" he shouted. And you know, Eben, it's not a good idea to dare the Lord!

The sailors were fixing to gather down below to decide what to do. As they walked away from the cabin, they saw something coming toward them, glowing like foxfire out in the piney woods. Oh, it was a horrible thing with fiery red eyes. It walked toward them, then it walked right through them and on into the captain's cabin, without bothering to open the door! It was a ghost . . . or maybe something even worse.

Uncle Dutch says they could hear the captain talking, like he was having a conbersation, but they could only hear one voice.

"I want no help! I need no help! Now get off my ship!" the captain shouted.

There were three gunshots. *Pow-pow-pow!* They heard a weird voice, like the wind howling. "This ship is doomed. And you are doomed to remain on board for all eternity!" Uncle Dutch says that means forever and ever.

The words gave my uncle an awful chill. The sailors broke down the door, and they were surprised as could be to see Captain Graves standing there with his pistol in one hand and an empty bottle in the other. It was this same bottle, Eben, and there was no one else in the room! Not a sign of another living soul.

There was a crash—*boom!*—and the ship pitched over on its side. Uncle Dutch says he slid right out the little round window called the "pothole" and over the edge of the ship. The next thing he knew, he was in the water, hanging on to a piece of floating wood. After a while the clouds lifted, and out popped a full moon with a big smiling face. The storm was over.

Uncle Dutch says he doesn't know how long he floated. Sometime the next day he reached land. He couldn't believe his good luck! He crawled onshore and looked around for other signs of life, but he never saw another sailor from that ship again. He spent the day there, and that afternoon he found something else that had floated onshore. It was this bottle and inside was this ship, just like you see it now, with these letters on the side saying, S.S. *Phantom of the Sea*. And you'd better believe that, Eben, or you'll be sorry.

Uncle Dutch says he wandered for a while until he found a village. Some Englishmen helped him get a place on a ship coming back home.

Since he got back, he's never so much as set foot in a canoe. He won't even get in the bathtub! He says nothing makes him happier than a hot summer day, the drier the better. He gave me this bottle 'cause he said he never wanted sight of it again. He told me to take special care of it.

"Don't ever break it, Rae Ellen," he said. "I can't be 'sponsible for what would happen if all that evil ever got out."

———

Rae Ellen stopped talking long enough for me to figure out the story was over. "It's a one-of-a-kind Wonderful, isn't it?" she asked.

"It's a good story," I said. "And it could be a Won-der. I might get to Colorado yet."

"Colorado!" Rae Ellen screeched. "Well, what do I get? It's my story! What are you going to give me for it?"

I considered for a moment. "I'll give you my pie on the first day of school." At least then she wouldn't have to steal it.

"First week," she insisted. "Five whole days."

I was in no mood to argue. "First week," I agreed. "And if I were you, Rae Ellen, I'd take real good care of that bottle . . . just in case."

When we came outside again, it was dark, and Pa insisted on driving Rae Ellen home in the pickup. That was a Wonder, because Pa wasn't one to waste gas. In fact, some folks didn't even know we had a truck, he used it so seldom.

He made me ride along, but I don't think any of us said a word all the way to the Hubbells' place. I kept a close eye on that burlap sack.

On the way back home, big fat raindrops started plopping on the windshield.

"Looks like your friend brought us luck," said Pa.

I didn't believe that, but I was feeling pretty certain she'd brought me a genuine Wonder.

## Days Six and Seven
# I Start Again

It poured rain on Monday—like the monsoon rains in India I read about in Hardy T. Lang's book. The weather was good for the crops but not good for Wonders. On the other hand, folks wouldn't be able to get out and trade stories about me getting tipped over in the outhouse for a while.

Even with the rain, the cows needed milking, the chickens needed feeding, and Aunt Pretty needed someone to stir the catsup she was making, and to taste it as well.

Pa thought it was fine weather to mend the fence, but when he came in from lunch, dripping like a drenched cat, he admitted that it might be a good afternoon to sit inside and balance his accounts.

"I thought of going down to the store, but there's a lake in the middle of Yellow Dog Road," he explained.

"Taste this." Aunt Pretty stuck a wooden spoon dripping with catsup in Pa's mouth.

"Good as ever," said Pa. "Will you be making chili sauce, too?"

"As if there's ever been a year I didn't," said Aunt Pretty. "Is it a tad on the sweet side?"

"Well, I like it sweet," said Pa.

Pa chewed on the sandwich Aunt Pretty set down before him. "Guess this weather's put a crimp in the Wonders business."

"Yep." I didn't want to talk about it.

"Still, you say you got five Wonders in five days. Not bad."

"But if I don't get out today, I'll have to get two of them tomorrow."

Aunt Pretty ladled catsup into the waiting jars. "Seems to me the boy could have a break on account of rain."

Pa considered that thought for a bit. "If I give him an extra day, he'll take an extra day. Let's leave it at seven and see what he comes up with."

My aunt sighed, but Pa acted like he didn't hear her and went back to eating. So did I.

Later, when the catsup didn't need tasting and Pa was going over figures in a big black book he kept, I did some accounting myself.

Five Wonders, or even six, weren't worth a thing. I'd uncovered some amazing things, but I'd stirred up some trouble as well. I wasn't certain if I could find two other Wonders, and I didn't know if I wanted to try anyway.

I drew up a map of Sassafras Springs and marked off all the farms and houses I knew of. Then I made a list of all the families I knew and checked off everyone I'd visited or talked to so far.

I was hoping when I had everything written down, it'd be clear what my next step would be. There'd be some place I'd forgotten that would clearly have a Wonder or two sitting around collecting dust.

"Why, I'd almost forgotten that ancient temple in the apple orchard," somebody would say. "And I think there's a Trojan Horse right next to it."

The Trojan Horse was something I wished I could see, but it was long gone. Imagine a wooden horse so big that the whole Greek army could get inside as a trick to get into Troy and fight their enemies.

The only trick we'd had in Sassafras Springs recently took place at the old outhouse in the woods. I didn't want to think about that again.

My list showed that there were some scattered spots I'd missed. The rest of the houses in town, all grouped around the Saylors' place. The rest of Bent Fork (but I'd be surprised if anybody but Calvin Smiley could come up with a Wonder). The east side of the ridge. The Bowies lived there, but Albert would have told me by now if they had a Wonder. There were a couple of other farms. The mayor lived up there, but I hated to bother such an important person. Then there was a spot where the ridge dropped off into Rooster Hollow, where Uncle Alf Dee lived. He raised prize-winning mules there, and it would take a mule to get down the steep rocky trail to his place. No wonder I'd put that one off so far.

It was a small list, and not too promising, but I never would have guessed Rae Ellen had a Wonder either. I decided if it wasn't raining the next day, I'd give it another try.

By suppertime I had my list, Pa's books were balanced, and we had thirty-six jars of catsup lined up on the windowsills.

It rained until dawn on Tuesday, or so Pa told me later. As soon as the sun was due to rise, the downpour stopped. I didn't see it myself, because I was still sleeping. I'd been getting out of bed at sunrise my whole life, but for some reason, that morning I slept in and no one woke me up.

I was wide awake, though, when I went into the kitchen for breakfast and saw that Aunt Pretty wasn't alone. Sitting at the kitchen table, as if he ate there every day, was Coogie Jackson, digging into a plate of biscuits and ham gravy.

"There's our sleepyhead," Aunt Pretty greeted me.

"Howdy, Eben." Coogie grinned.

"What are you doing here?" I guess I didn't sound overly friendly.

"Calm down," said Coogie. "I'm here to make up for what happened the other day."

I slid into my seat at the table, and Aunt Pretty set down a plate for me.

"I was just having fun." Coogie stopped to take a

big gulp of milk. "Jeb said how important this Wonder thing was to you, so I'm here to help you."

"Help me what?"

"Find those last two Wonders. Jeb's coming too."

Jeb had talked to Coogie about me? I guess he was still my best friend, even if he didn't understand about exploring and Wonders and such.

I glanced over at Aunt Pretty. "I'm supposed to find them on my own."

"Land's sake, nobody said a friend couldn't point one out to you," she said. "Why, that Rae Ellen brought one right to your door."

Just what I didn't want Coogie to hear. But it turns out he knew already. "That's right. If Rae Ellen has a Wonder, anybody can have one."

"But Pa needs me to work."

"He went down to pick up the mail, Eben, but he said to tell you that you have the whole day off," Aunt Pretty announced proudly.

Everybody was acting mighty peculiar. I was trying to figure it out when Coogie wiped his mouth with a napkin and pushed his chair back. "Miss McAllister, you are the best cook in the county," he said. "Just like everybody says."

"Can't you stay for seconds?" My aunt sounded kind of wistful.

"No, ma'am," he answered. "Not on a two-Wonder day."

I shoveled in another mouthful of biscuit and pushed my chair back too.

As we left Coogie told my aunt, "Better not expect him for lunch."

Sal was out the door before we were, as usual.

We stopped by the Austins' place to pick up Jeb. "Don't you have to look after your brothers and sisters?" I asked.

"Nope," said Jeb. "Guess this is some kind of holiday."

I looked at Jeb and Coogie. "No tricks?"

"Just Wonders," said Coogie.

It seems that Coogie and Jeb thought finding Wonders was like picking apples—the more people you had, the faster you could gather them.

It seems that they were wrong.

If you ever want to learn about your neighbors, just go asking them for Wonders. You'll learn more than any census or government survey will ever tell you. Here's what I found out that day:

—On the whole, folks don't like to open their doors to barefoot boys in dusty overalls (which makes Lily Saylor a Wonder in herself, because she not only let us in her fancy house and showed us her valuables, she gave us chocolate).

—On the whole, rich or poor, most folks believe they are in possession of a Wonder, whether it's their grandfather's glass eye, a silver spoon from the Palace of Electricity at the 1904 World's Fair, or a pumpkin that's a dead ringer for Abe Lincoln. (And I'll say, that long, skinny pumpkin was every bit as awesome as a little pearl that comes from an oyster aggravated by a grain of sand.)

—On the whole, folks have a hard time saying that they don't own anything special, so you can fritter away a considerable amount of time looking at knives with broken blades, faded lace doilies, or recipes for moonshine. And on that last subject, my lips are sealed.

So what started out like a lark (at least in Coogie's mind) ended up being a job. It seems before we knew it, it was afternoon and we hadn't found a Wonder . . . or had a bite to eat. Coogie's idea of skipping lunch was not working out.

"Why don't you go on home?" I told Jeb, who was holding his stomach and moaning with hunger.

"Because I promised I wouldn't quit until we had two Wonders," he said.

"You didn't promise me," I told him.

"I know, but I promised myself."

"I'm not quitting," said Coogie. "But if somebody had a Wonder that included fried chicken, I wouldn't be sorry," he admitted.

I was too grateful for his help to suggest he eat a June bug. Those days were over for both of us.

"What's left?" Coogie rubbed his belly with both hands.

I looked at my list. "I did the town and the hollow, you and Jeb covered the Peeveys and the Cuthberts. Oh, we haven't seen Uncle Alf Dee."

"I can't make it all the way down to Rooster Hollow! I'll faint from hunger," said Jeb.

Coogie glanced up the hill. "How about a water-melon to tide us over?"

"Watermelon!" Jeb moaned. "Don't torture me."

One watermelon can fill up three boys in a hurry. And Coogie had just spotted a mess of ripe water-melons on the hillside.

"Stealing's no good," I told them. I was quite sure those watermelons weren't growing wild.

"How're we going to cut it?" Jeb asked, as if he hadn't heard me.

"With a rock. I know how," said Coogie. I guess he hadn't heard me either.

I gave in, figuring nobody would miss one water-melon out of so many. "Be quick about it."

Coogie thumped two or three of the biggest melons, then made his selection. Jeb found a rock.

"Not out here in the open," I said.

The two of them picked up the watermelon and carried it toward a stand of trees, while I scanned the hillside for witnesses. I didn't see a soul, so I almost fainted when I felt a firm hand on my shoulder.

A deep bass voice spoke. "Boy, I want to talk to you."

I slowly turned to face Marvin Peevey, the elected and respected mayor of Sassafras Springs.

"Come with me."

Sal wagged her tail but I didn't. I knew I was caught red-handed. There was no arguing with the mayor, who counted the county sheriff as a close friend. As Sal and I followed him up the hill, moving toward his farm, I looked around but saw no sign of Coogie, Jeb, or the missing watermelon.

Since Sassafras Springs is small, being in charge of it doesn't pay much, so Mayor Peevey continued to farm full-time. Still, Pa always told me that the mayor was a man to be respected. "He's as upright as the preacher," said Pa. "Maybe even more so."

Mayor Peevey never looked back at me, but there was no point in me running away. He and Pa were pretty close, and I'd get found out sooner or later if I ran.

Once we got to his farm, the mayor spun around and looked me in the eye.

"Now I want to know the truth."

The truth was, I didn't steal the watermelon, but a judge would call me an "accessory to the crime." Which means I was guilty anyway.

"Yes, sir."

"Why on God's green earth did you ask everybody in Sassafras Springs for a Wonder except me?"

I was struck dumb by that question, since I thought this conversation was going to be about watermelons, not Wonders, but somehow I found my voice.

"I believe Jeb Austin asked Mrs. Peevey this morning."

Mayor Peevey glanced toward the farmyard where Mrs. Peevey, the First Lady of Sassafras Springs, was carrying slops to the hogs. The Peeveys raised hogs fine enough to give the Bowies competition.

"Sometimes you can have a Wonder right under your nose," he said. "But if you don't know the meaning of it, it's worthless."

Without a word of explanation, he walked toward his house.

A voice rang out. "Mind your manners now!"

I jumped, but it was just Mrs. Peevey talking to her rambunctious hogs.

A minute later the mayor came back outside carrying something under his arm. "A boy like you might benefit from seeing this," he said.

He unrolled a huge piece of blue-and-gray fabric and held it up. Big red letters woven into the cloth spelled out BUDDY across the center.

"Who's Buddy?" I asked.

"You'll find out in good time. Now, this may seem like an ordinary old piece of cloth with a name on it. But when you hear how it was made . . . Eben, you'd better sit while I tell you."

The mayor and I settled down on a couple of old log ends set up like stools. Sal picked out a patch of shade and lay down for a nap. I guess she sensed another story coming on.

# Mayor Peevey's Story

## Song of the Loom

*Back when I was growing up, there were a few ornery youngsters around Sassafras Springs who gave folks a terrible time, but the worst of those children was a boy named Buddy. Now, there may have been reasons why Buddy acted up. He had no mother and his father drank. And when he drank, he got mean. Still, the boy had been to Sunday school, and he knew right from wrong. Most folks do.*

Late one night those boys and girls, led by Buddy, crawled in the schoolteacher's window, stole his trousers, and sewed the legs together. They sneaked back in and laid those trousers back over his chair, neatly folded. In the morning you could hear the teacher yelling for miles around. He'd put on his trousers, tried to take a step and toppled over. He hit his head on the bedpost and got a dandy black eye. There was no school for a week. No one minded missing a week of school, I've got to say. Still, that was a pretty mean trick. Even though the schoolteacher blamed Buddy, nobody had any proof, so Buddy went unpunished. That just encouraged him to keep up his reputation as the number one scalawag in Sassafras Springs.

One night Buddy talked a few friends into tying Old Man Munson's brand-new buggy up in the branches of a tree. Mr. Munson was so proud of that thing, he washed and polished it every day till it glowed in the dark. When he saw his expensive beauty dangling from the tree, the old man flew into a rage. He grabbed his scythe and cut the thing down, which is exactly what Buddy hoped he'd do. He watched from the woods, laughing like a lunatic, as that fancy new buggy crashed to the ground and broke into a hundred pieces. Old Man Munson had some kind of fit and ran off into the woods, screaming. He was never quite sure who'd played that dirty trick on him in the first place. Though, of course, everyone suspected Buddy.

Anyway, you can see how Buddy got to be known as the worst boy in Sassafras Springs, even though no one ever caught him in the act, not once. Until he tried to play a trick on Old Emma.

Everybody in Sassafras Springs called her Old Emma, and she was definitely old. She was also blind, completely blind. She lived with her daughter, Lulu, and Lulu's family, and all day long Old Emma sat at her loom, weaving cloth. Now, that might sound like a funny thing for a blind person to do, but Old Emma hadn't always been blind. She said her fingers still remembered what to do.

How she'd thread that loom, her not seeing a thing, no one ever knew. She'd thread it and throw the shuttle and start working the foot treadles. Weaving's like playing the organ, the way you move your feet on those pedals. And once Old Emma got the loom going, it practically sang a song for her.

"Warp and woof, warp and woof. Shoot the shuttle back and forth. Warp and woof, warp and woof. Lock it, roll it, start again." That's how it went, I recall.

Her weaving looked good, too. She still remembered what colors and patterns looked like. And she always said the loom told her what colors to put where. It may not make sense, but if you'd seen her weaving, you'd believe it.

Old Emma liked to keep her independence, so Lulu fixed up ropes leading from the house out to the shed, where she kept her loom, and another one from the shed out to the privy. Old Emma would grab on to the ropes and feel her way along until she got where she wanted to go. That way, she didn't have to ask anybody for help.

One day Buddy got a notion that he thought was funny. Fact is, it was just plain mean. When it was dark, Buddy sneaked over, untied those ropes, and fixed them so they led way out into the woods. Then he added more ropes and built a kind of a maze that looped around all the trees. He meant to confuse her, but he got more than he bargained for.

At the crack of dawn, as was her habit, Old Emma started out to the shed. She followed those ropes round this tree and that. Instead of working her way back to the house like Buddy had figured, she got all tangled up in the bushes, then twisted her ankle and fell. She screamed till she was hoarse. When her folks finally found her, her teeth were chattering, and she was scared half to death, poor woman.

Who could have done such a thing? Nobody would own up to it, especially not Buddy. He said he'd been home reading a book the teacher gave him. He told the whole story of that book to prove it, and he was convincing.

"I'll find the truth of who did it," Old Emma told everybody she talked to. "The loom will tell me. I'll weave a piece of cloth that will tell me exactly who's guilty."

When Buddy heard that, he got a mite nervous. The next night he sneaked into Old Emma's shed, and he got into her bobbins of thread; they were big rolls of thread in all different colors. She kept them in order so she'd know which color to put on next. Buddy mixed them all up. He figured whatever she wove would be gibberish because the colors wouldn't be the way she wanted them.

The next morning Old Emma went out to the shed and started weaving. She wove all day, and when her daughter came out to tell her it was lunchtime, she wouldn't stop. "The loom is singing to me, Lulu," she told her. "The loom knows the secret and it will tell me the truth."

Later Lulu came out to tell her mother it was

time for supper, but Old Emma wouldn't stop weaving. "I can't interrupt the song of the loom," she said. Lulu brought her a basket of food, because she knew once her mother got an idea in her head, nothing would change her mind.

Old Emma wove all night long. Buddy sneaked by, and he could see her silhouette in the moonlight through the window, sitting in the pitch dark, weaving away.

That sight gave Buddy the jimjams. And well it should have.

The next morning, when Lulu and her family got up, Old Emma was sitting in the kitchen with a cloth rolled up on her lap. "I'm finished," she said. "I'll see that the guilty one is punished now. You'll have to read me what it says."

She held up the cloth—this cloth I showed you— and Lulu saw the big red letters. They spelled out BUDDY.

Old Emma insisted that Lulu take her over to Buddy's house. She banged at the door and woke up his pa. That took quite a while, since he was sleeping off a bottle of moonshine, as usual. She kept banging on the door, and when he opened it, she

told Buddy's pa what had happened. Then she showed him the cloth. Buddy watched from the shadows, sweating.

"What do you have to say for yourself, young man?" Old Emma asked.

When Buddy saw his name in big red letters, his knees got all weak. Mixing up the yarn hadn't done a thing, because the loom knew he did it. And Old Emma had heard the song of the loom.

"I'm sorry," he said. "I fooled with those ropes as a joke. But I'm sorry I did."

"You're no dang good!" his father shrieked as he rolled up his sleeves. "I'll beat some sense into you."

"No!" said Old Emma in a voice so loud, it shut Buddy's pa right up.

"Did you say you're sorry?" she asked the boy.

"As sorry as a person can be." Buddy's voice was shaking.

"Sorry enough that you're not ever going to do anything bad to anybody again?" Old Emma asked.

"Yes, ma'am," said Buddy. His voice cracked. "I'm only going to help folks from now on. I promise."

"He's no good!" the father argued.

"No," said Old Emma. "I believe him. In fact, I

believe he could be the most helpful person in Sassafras Springs. The loom told me so."

Old Emma handed Buddy the cloth and told him to keep it always so he wouldn't forget. And the Wonder of it all isn't that the word appeared here or that his pa didn't beat him. The Wonder is that Buddy never did anything bad to anybody again. He spent every day since then trying to help folks. Now that, my boy, is a Wonder that's higher than your highest pyramid and deeper than your deep blue seas. That is a Wonder of Sassafras Springs.

———

That was one whale of a story all right, but I didn't know of anybody in Sassafras Springs called Buddy. "How'd you end up with this cloth, Mayor?" I asked.

"I told you, young man. Old Emma gave it to me and it changed my life," said the mayor.

I gasped. "You don't mean you're—"

"I'm Marvin Peevey, son. Growing up, everybody in Sassafras Springs called me Buddy. Ask your pa."

I shook my head. "I can't believe you did such awful things!"

"Neither can I," said the mayor. "I didn't think I

was being mean. I thought I was smarter than other folks. I was so smart, I was a smart aleck, I'll tell you. But on that day, I saw that I could use my brains to do good things too. I saw the light, Eben. I keep this cloth hanging on my wall to remind me that there are some things you can't hide, so you might as well be honest."

"I'd call that a Wonder!" I said.

By doggies, I could hear the train whistle calling me to Colorado, feel the tug of the wheels pulling the cars up a mountain.

Still, something was bothering me.

"Mayor Peevey, I guess I have to tell you, I did something pretty bad today, and I don't want to hide it."

The mayor raised one eyebrow and waited.

"My friends and I helped ourselves to one of your watermelons over on the hill. We were powerful hungry, but it's still stealing, isn't it?"

The mayor stroked his chin. I waited . . . and waited some more. "One watermelon? I think we could call it even if you and your friends could give me an hour or two of chopping wood this week."

I was plain relieved. "Sounds fair."

But something else was still nagging at me. "Mayor Peevey, where'd that loom go, anyway?"

The mayor shrugged. "Don't know," he said. "I guess Uncle Alf Dee has it."

"Why's that?"

"Uncle Alf is Lulu's son. Old Emma was his grandmother. And if you need another Wonder, I advise you to pay him a visit. If you don't, you'll hear about it!"

Jeb and Coogie were waiting for me down on Yellow Dog Road.

"We thought you'd be locked up," said Coogie.

"We vowed to break you out of jail one way or another," Jeb added.

"It wasn't what you think. While you two were filling up on watermelon, I got myself the sixth Wonder!"

I enjoyed seeing the surprised look on their faces. They wanted to hear all about it, but I had no time to talk.

"I've got to get home to dinner."

"Can't it wait?" asked Coogie.

"No, sir. If I don't get something in my stomach soon, I'll fade away to nothing. I'll tell you the whole story when we're chopping wood for the mayor."

I left them in the middle of the road, looking confused, as Sal and I trotted home. I do believe that dog was at least as hungry as I was.

## Day Eight
# A Setback
# and a Surprise

No one mentioned Wonders during dinner, though Pa did marvel when I put away my third helping of dumplings. After the dishes were washed and put away, Pa and I sat on the porch in silence, until Aunt Pretty bustled out to join us. Her arms were full of clothes. "Here's your traveling outfit, Eben," she said with pride. "Just like brand-new. Now stand up, and let's see if these things will fit."

There was a first-rate shirt, a pair of trousers that looked brand-new, knitted socks, and store-bought suspenders that must have been bought out of Aunt Pretty's pin money. The clothes fit fine and Aunt Pretty even said I looked handsome.

"It's the seventh day, you know," I said.

"I happened to look at the calendar today," said Pa.

"I've got one more Wonder to find, and I think I can do it"—I took a deep breath—"if you could see clear to giving me one more day."

I waited for a big reaction, but Pa just leaned back and closed his eyes.

"Makes sense to me," said Aunt Pretty, folding up my new duds. "The Lord may have created the earth in six days with one to spare, but he didn't have to help his pa in the fields."

Pa cleared his throat. I knew that meant he had something more important on his mind. "Eben, I've always been honest with you, or tried to be. That's why I've got to show you this letter that came from Cousin Molly today."

He reached into his shirt pocket, pulled out a letter, and held it out for me to take. I guess I didn't want to know what was in that letter, because my hand wouldn't take it.

Pa paused to tell me he'd written to Molly to ask if I could stay with them. Then he carefully unfolded the letter and read it out loud.

*"Dear Cousin Cole,*

*Thank you for the letter. Although we'd love to have Eben visit, this is not a good time as the whole town of Silver Peak is down with influenza. Many have died. Eli almost met his Maker but pulled through, for which I am grateful. Maybe next year your boy could come see us. Hello to your sister.*

*Sincerely,*

*Molly Campbell."*

"I told you that place was not fit for humans," Aunt Pretty remarked, plopping down into her rocker. "Influenza!"

"Now, Pretty, this is a big disappointment to the boy," Pa told her.

My heart crashed down to my toes and my eyes got blurry. Disappointment? I'll say! I'd frittered away the better part of a week and now that dream of a mountain had just crumbled to dust.

"I guess it doesn't matter about the seventh Wonder, because I can't make good on my promise." Pa sounded as disappointed as I felt.

Aunt Pretty patted my arm. "Next year will be here soon enough. Then you can go." Surprisingly, she chuckled. "Say, you certainly got folks worked up about Wonders! I haven't seen so much excitement around here for years. Since that carnival came, I think."

My voice came back. "Maybe they weren't Wonders after all." I hadn't figured out how an applehead doll measured up to a pyramid or how a musical saw stacked up to the Hanging Gardens of Babylon.

"Why not let us be the judge of that?" said Pa.

So I took out my tablet and read them all my stories, adding a few details here and there as I described all I'd heard and seen.

Pa and Aunt Pretty and even Sal listened in silence, except for an occasional "My word," or "I never heard that!" from my aunt, who stopped crocheting entirely by the third Wonder.

When I was finished, Pa said, "Those were rip-roaring stories, all right. Say, I met Dutch Hubbell once. He looked like he'd seen a ghost. His hair stood straight up all the time."

"And I'd forgotten what a bad boy Buddy Peevey was," my aunt added.

I sat there, thinking about the Wonders as the evening shadows settled over the barnyard. A doll. A bookcase. A saw. A table. A ship in a bottle. A woven cloth. They were all as unimpressive and ordinary as Sassafras Springs, yet each in its own way was a one-of-a-kind marvel.

After the light was gone, Aunt Pretty stood up and gave me a strange look, then abruptly went inside the house without a word. A little while later, she came back out toting a lantern and a big shoe box. "Now, I know these are no Wonders. In fact they're about as ordinary as can be. But if Mrs. Pritchard can show off some dried-up apple doll and Violet Rowan can brag about a worn-out table, you might as well see these."

She took the lid off and turned the box on its side. Out tumbled a whole world of little people, all dressed up and painted and made of clothespins. Someone had painted faces on the round tops, and they were dressed in overalls, or suits, or dresses— even a preacher's outfit.

"What are they?" I asked.

"These are my clothespin people. When I was a girl, my very best friend and I used to make them. That

Cally, she had a sense of humor." Aunt Pretty held up a doll that had a grizzled-fur beard and stuffing around the middle. "Isn't this the spitting image of old Ev Olson?" she asked Pa. He nodded and chuckled.

She held up another one, dressed in leather. "I made this Indian, and Cally did the preacher." She displayed another figure with a flowered dress and a gigantic hat. "Cally and I liked to split our sides laughing at this hat Lessie wore to the church social."

"Aunt Pretty, these are wonderful! Look, there's a pilgrim. And a Santa Claus."

"We had a lot of fun, but we stopped when we were grown up. Once Cally moved away, I went back to making them, just so's I'd never forget. Every wash day while I'm hanging clothes, one clothespin seems to suddenly look just like somebody I know, and there I go again. 'Course they're no Wonders of the World, but they help me remember Cally."

I sure hoped she wasn't going to start crying. Instead she reached into her pocket and pulled out another clothespin person. It was a boy wearing a tiny shirt, trousers, and suspenders that exactly matched the outfit my aunt had just made me.

"It's me, Aunt Pretty. Doesn't that beat all!"

"I thought it might bring you luck on your trip."

Without another word, my aunt whisked her entire clothespin population back into the box and went into the house.

"That Pretty, she's the one who's a Wonder," Pa said admiringly. I had no trouble agreeing with that.

When Pa finally rose to go into the house, I had a question for him. "Think I could have an hour off tomorrow, if I start an hour early?"

"Have to get your own breakfast. Have to coax Mabel and Myrt into giving up some milk an hour early," said Pa.

"I'll do it." The cows might be cranky, but they were never in that good a mood anyway.

"Are you going to look for that seventh Wonder?" he asked.

"Yessir, I believe I will."

You'd think after a week of searching for Wonders, Sal would be getting a mite bored. But she didn't mind a bit as we made our way down the winding, rocky trail that led to Alf Dee's mule farm. I found it slow going, though. You'd have to be a mule—or mule-headed—to make it, but we did.

Strangely enough, Uncle Alf was standing on his tidy white porch when I got there, like he'd been waiting for me.

"Hurry on in here now, son," he called to me as I hurried up his garden path. I speeded up as Sal dashed ahead, squeezing through the screen door before me.

"'Bout time you got here," Uncle Alf greeted me.

"You were expecting me?"

"Word gets around Sassafras Springs, Eben. I know you need a seventh Wonder and I might have one for you. Only you can be the judge of that," Uncle Alf answered. "Dog, you lay down there." He pointed to a rug by the front door. Sal did just what he said. Everybody listened to Uncle Alf. He was nobody's uncle that anybody knew of, but folks respected him.

Alfred Dee stood as straight as a fence post, and he wore the Sassafras Springs uniform: a rough blue shirt and worn overalls with a red bandanna sticking out of the back pocket. He was stick thin, with cheekbones like rocky mountain peaks that rose above a droopy brown mustache.

Folks had been calling him Uncle Alf for years, even though he was barely older than Pa. He'd been married once but his wife died young, before they had a chance to have a family. That's when he became "Uncle Alf" to everyone else's children.

Inside, his house was neat and clean. The only unusual thing was what was sitting on the dining-room table—and believe me, it wasn't dinner! The sight of it purely took my breath away because spread out before me was all of Sassafras Springs—every inch of it—in miniature.

"It's  it's Sassafras Springs!" I exclaimed. "How'd you do it?"

"Carved it all with my own two hands. It's only taken most of my life so far. And it's not finished yet. Not by a long shot."

I bent down for a closer look. It was all there—all carved and nailed, all glued and painted. All the houses and the farms, with Yellow Dog Road pointing the way through the middle of town and out again.

I saw our house—small and white and neat, and its big white porch with the floor painted dark green. A miniature Aunt Pretty sat in her chair, holding a toothpick-size crochet hook.

A tiny Pa sat on the steps with a boy reading a thick book.

"That's my Seven Wonders book," I burst out. That scene had taken place only a few nights ago!

"You don't say," murmured Uncle Alf.

I followed the whole layout up Yellow Dog Road to the ridge and the Pritchard cottage. Mrs. Pritchard, dead-on perfect to the flowers blooming on her dress, was hanging laundry. Farther up the road, Cully Pone's shack had a familiar slant to its roof. A three-inch Cully stood poised over an old stump, ready to lower the blade of his ax.

The church was surrounded by trees and tombstones. Through colored cellophane panels on the church windows, I could see Calvin Smiley holding a bow over his musical saw.

"This all just happened!" I could hardly breathe.

Eulie and Violet Rowan tended their garden; Rae Ellen stood outside our barn, holding a burlap sack that glowed eerily. I pulled back.

The rest of Sassafras Springs was just as real. Lessie Mull in her yellow sunbonnet. Grandma Mayer had put up a jar of pickles. Mayor Peevey hoed potatoes while the First Lady slopped toy hogs. Lily Saylor stood on her porch, clutching a red satin box close to her heart.

"How do you see it? You weren't there. How'd you know what happened?" I asked.

Uncle Alf shrugged his bony shoulders. "Can't rightly say, Eben. When I get to carving, I start seeing how things are, that's all. I guess my grandmother Emma was the same way with that loom of hers. I can tell you about the carving, if you want to hear it."

I wanted to hear it. I knew when I was face-to-face with a genuine Wonder. And even if it wasn't, I still wanted to know the secret of Uncle Alf's carvings.

# Uncle Alf's Story

## Graven Images

*When I was your age, I wanted to carve wood but I didn't know how. Most men whittled toys and whistles, but nobody I knew could carve a real figure. I had me a knife that I kept real sharp, and in my spare time I'd practice. Nothing ever came out quite right.*

One day a traveling artist came through Sassafras Springs. His name was LaFlame and from the way he talked, he was a genuine Frenchman. He'd paint your portrait for five dollars. Everybody wanted one; only a few could afford it. One family had him paint a colored copy of a photo of their little girl who had died. He made her look like an angel. The town board got together five dollars to paint the picture of the mayor . . . Hobart was his name.

THE SEVEN WONDERS OF SASSAFRAS SPRINGS

Everybody was kind of puzzled because he came out looking more like a devil, and it turned out he was. Ran off with some funds, I recall. Anyway, the church hired LaFlame to paint some angels on the ceiling. He had angels flying all over that place—beautiful ones. They've been painted over since then. Seems some committee decided they were too fanciful for an ordinary country church.

One night he stopped by to see if my ma would buy a picture. She didn't have five dollars, but she gave him a glass of cool water. He was resting on the porch when he saw me with the knife and wood. He asked what I was trying to do with it.

When I told him, LaFlame laughed at me and said I was going about it all wrong. He said you can't just start in carving. You've got to get to know the wood, let it get to know you. You've got to hold the wood, warm to it, feel the beat of its pulse.

He took that wood and he rolled it around in his hands, like he was kneading bread dough. After a while, he took my knife and showed me how to make deep cuts, not just hack away at it. I watched him real careful-like for a while.

All of a sudden he stood up and handed the wood to me. "You're ready for it now," he told me. And with that, LaFlame walked off the porch and right out of Sassafras Springs forever.

I kept on carving anyway, without knowing what I was doing. When I was finished, I laughed out loud, because I'd carved myself an angel without even knowing it! All because that angel artist had worked the wood for me. Pretty angel it was, but I never carved another angel again.

Some years later I was at a dance and met a pretty gal from Blue River. I felt for certain that I'd seen her before. When I got home, I rushed upstairs and got that wooden angel out of a drawer and there she was. The face was the spitting image of that gal, like a photograph.

Of course, I married her. And I've been carving ever since.

Now, I won't try to explain what I just said, because I don't understand it. I don't have to understand it. I just have to do the carving. The wood does the rest.

_____

It was far-fetched, but looking at that miniature version of my home town, I'd have believed anything.

A worry was growing somewhere in my head as I studied the layout again. Sassafras Springs was there in every up-to-the-moment detail. There were odd things too. A woman with a dog and a lantern approached a man sitting at a table in the graveyard. A cottony cloud of locusts hovered over a farm where a tiny family raised brooms in the fields. On the far edge was an outcropping of rocks, high above a creek, where a man in a top hat tended a fire. And out in a shed behind a farmhouse, an old woman sat before a loom.

"You've got the past and the present all mixed up," I told Uncle Alf.

"The older you get, the more the past and the present are all mixed up in your brain," Uncle Alf patiently explained. "Future too, I guess."

I pointed to the end of Yellow Dog Road, where I noticed a funny figure, kind of like me, though older somehow. He was on the edge of Sassafras Springs, walking away from town. He had a small suitcase in one hand and a scruffy old dog following him.

"Who's that?"

"Who does it look like?"

"It's . . . me." I could barely whisper what I was thinking. "It looks like I'm leaving. Is that it?"

"Kind of looks that way to me, too."

I swallowed hard. I'd said often enough that I'd get out of Sassafras Springs some day. Seeing myself walking down that road with no one stopping me made me feel kind of funny inside. Glad and sad and kind of lonely.

I remembered what Aunt Pretty said. "I hope the farm doesn't go to rack and ruin," I repeated.

"Not likely. And it doesn't mean you'll never come back," Uncle Alf said softly. "Seems as if you're off to see the world. 'Course, up to now, I had my doubts."

"What do you mean?"

"Eben, there are two kinds of folks: those who are satisfied right where they are and those with an itch to see the rest of the world. If you're the kind who's got to go, then get going. Even if you don't, now that you've found seven Wonders, I'll bet you'll be noticing new ones every day."

Uncle Alf held out his fist and opened his fingers to reveal an unfinished carving of a baby.

"Who's that?" I asked.

"Don't know yet. Don't know whether it's a boy or girl. We'll all know in due time," Uncle Alf said.

I looked down at that tiny Sassafras Springs and I thought about Junior's egg and Lessie Mull's log cabin quilt, Mrs. Saylor's jade bracelet and Aunt Pretty's green glass beads, Eulie Rowan's worn table and Calvin Smiley's ordinary saw. "I was only looking for big things," I told him. "But a small thing can be a prize too."

"You have something there, boy."

I straightened up and pulled out my tablet. "Well, I've found the seventh Wonder. Maybe not of the whole world . . . but it's the Seventh Wonder of Sassafras Springs for sure."

"Could be," answered Uncle Alf. "And Eben . . ."

Uncle Alf glanced down at that tiny baby-to-be in his hand. "Please say hello to your Aunt Pretty for me. I would be pleased if she stopped by some day."

"Yes, sir." Something else was bothering me. "Uncle Alf? Do you still have your grandma's loom?"

"Not exactly, Eben." Uncle Alf spoke softly. "After

Grandmother died, that loom sat silent in the shed until one day a big wind came along and smashed the shed and the loom into a pile of sticks. I stacked it all up and I've been carving on it for years. Most of the carvings you see here came out of that loom. I think Grandmother would have like it that way."

Old Emma definitely would have liked it, I decided as I walked home, full of questions and confusion and, well, full of wonder.

## Day Nine
# Change of Plans

Aunt Pretty was so anxious to hear what I was up to, she pestered me all through dinner to tell her the story.

When I finally told her and Pa about Uncle Alf, she was even more interested. Especially after I said he'd asked about her.

"I never knew Alfred carved that little village. That would be something to see." Aunt Pretty sat on the edge of her rocker. Her hands were still for once.

"Alfred? You call him Alfred?" I was amazed.

"Goodness, I've known him my whole life," Aunt Pretty said. "I never saw that little village, though."

"Why don't you call on him, Pretty? I recall you two were friendly at one time," Pa suggested with a sly grin.

"I think I'll do that," Aunt Pretty declared. "I'll bake him an apple pie. I'll bet it's been years since Alfred had a homemade apple pie."

"It's a rough road to his house," I warned her. "You'd have to be a mule to make it."

Aunt Pretty laughed. "I've been down plenty of rough roads, Eben. And I'm as stubborn as a mule— you know that."

I could see she was determined. "Wear your blue dress when you go," I suggested. "I like that dress."

My aunt's face turned pink. "I'm just going to see the carvings. But maybe I'll see if that dress is clean."

She started to go inside, then came right back. "Lord, I got so caught up in hearing about Alfred, I forgot I had something important to tell you, Eben."

"What?"

"I went down and made a long-distance telephone call today," she announced proudly. That got my attention, since we didn't have a phone. The locals all went to Yount's General to make their calls. Hiram charged them a pretty penny to do so. But *long distance*!

"I called Cousin Lottie in St. Louis. She's our second cousin on my mother's side. She worked for some rich folks there, till she got married. Now she's got a house in the city and a couple of kids, younger than you, Eben. Anyway, she said she'd be plain delighted to have you visit her week after next. Says she misses having kinfolk around."

I couldn't believe the words coming out of Aunt Pretty's mouth.

"I haven't seen Lottie in years. Not since . . . the funeral," said Pa, lowering his voice at the thought of my mother's passing.

I remembered Cousin Lottie, big and friendly, with braids that wound around her head like friendly snakes.

"St. Louis," I half whispered. "Can I go, Pa?"

"Well, if your aunt went to all the trouble of making a phone call, I should say so. I can hire Buck Fielding to work for a couple of days. He's always happy to earn a little extra."

So there it was: St. Louis, Missouri! There had to be some Wonders of the World there. Why, they'd already had a World's Fair . . . and there were tall buildings and a zoo, museums and cathedrals and even the mighty, muddy Mississippi River, with a famous bridge across it. A fellow who'd been to St. Louis would never be the same again!

---

The next morning I woke up to the smell of apples and cinnamon drifting through my window. By the time I got downstairs for breakfast, Aunt Pretty was covering an apple pie with a towel. I saw that she was wearing her blue dress, freshly washed and ironed. And there was a brand-new band of crocheted lace around the collar.

"Thought I'd mosey on down to Alfred's early," she explained. "He could have some pie for breakfast."

"Maybe you ought to take along your clothespin people," Pa suggested.

"Not this time. Not yet," she said mysteriously. Then Pa did something else shocking: He offered her a ride in the pickup.

"No, thanks. I'll enjoy the walk," Aunt Pretty told him.

"Say howdy for me," Pa said. "You look mighty nice."

My stars, hard as it was to believe, as my aunt traveled down the road, she *did* look real nice. And if my aunt was actually pretty, well, that might be another Wonder of Sassafras Springs.

"Looks like Alf Dee's going to get your aunt's apple pie at last," said Pa, as he watched her walk away.

You could have knocked me over with a feather. "You mean, he was one of the ones who lost out to Holt?"

Pa just winked his answer.

Maybe Uncle Alf was carving up a wedding scene right now. After all, like Pa said, Aunt Pretty was still in her prime. Maybe Uncle Alf was going to be somebody's uncle after all. And that somebody could be me.

I hayed with Pa most all of the morning.

"That's a happy tune," Pa said as he tossed a pitchfork of hay up on the wagon, where I was waiting to spread it out.

I hadn't noticed I was whistling.

Later I laughed out loud when I gazed up at old Redhead Hill. From up there on the wagon, if you looked a certain way, the two houses on the hill appeared to be a pair of eyes staring out from under a mop of red hair.

"I never noticed that before," I told Pa.

He chuckled. "Depends on your point of view."

While Pa ate his lunch, I grabbed my sandwich and gobbled it down on the way to Jeb's house.

I couldn't wait a second longer to tell him the news.
He was out in the cornfield, eating lunch with
his brothers and sisters and his pa.
He ran up to meet me.
"I heard you're
going to St. Louis,"
he greeted me.
"Lucky you!"

I wanted to know how on Earth he could know that before I'd told a soul.

"Aw, everybody knows it. Your pa told Buck Fielding, and it spread from there. Say, Hiram Yount went to St. Louis once and said they've got streetcars going down the middle of the street that run on an electrical wire. Set off sparks everywhere—like redhot snowflakes!"

Red-hot snowflakes! Now that's a Wonder I didn't want to miss.

———

I worked extra hard the next week, maybe because I was hoping Pa would miss me when I was gone.

I already knew I'd miss him.

On the afternoon before I left, Sal stretched her legs and looked up at me hopeful-like. I could see she was itching to go searching for more Wonders.

"We're finished with all that now," I told her, but she just wagged her tail.

"Aw, I guess it won't hurt to keep looking," I said as she led me out to Yellow Dog Road and to more Wonders of Sassafras Springs.

# The Beginning

It was sunny the Saturday morning I left. My new clothes felt stiff and strange after a summer spent in overalls, but they looked fine, thanks to Aunt Pretty.

Thanks to Pa, I had some folding money in my pocket.

With tears welling up in her eyes, my aunt gave me a lunch bucket to take on the train. "I never thought you'd grow up so fast," she said, wiping her eyes with her apron. She tucked one of her crocheted scarves in my pocket. "Something for Cousin Lottie."

"Don't worry, Aunt Pretty. I'll be back. I'll always come back to see you."

Pa climbed into the front seat of the pickup and Aunt Pretty slid in next to him. Sal and I jumped in the open back with my new suitcase, a gift from Uncle Alf.

"I believe you'll give it quite a bit of use," he'd told me.

As the truck coasted down Yellow Dog Road, I was surprised to see so many people out. Violet and Eulie Rowan, carrying their baskets of herbs, paused to wave to me. As we passed the Austins', I didn't see Jeb, but his brothers and sisters were all sitting on the fence, waving. Pa honked the horn.

Farther down the road, I saw Cully Pone shaking his moth-eaten hat in our direction. Up on the hill, Mayor Peevey stopped plowing in his field to wave his big straw hat.

And there were others, just waiting by the side of the road. The Bowie brothers and Piggy Ellis, Buck Fielding and Lessie Mull.

When we reached town, Lily Saylor stood on her porch, waving a white handkerchief at me. She had roses pinned in her hair.

It was like I was riding in a big parade, but I was the only attraction that day.

Pa stopped to fill up at the gas pumps in front of the general store, and Hiram Yount was panting a bit as he rushed outside to help.

"So you're going after all," he said. "Always knew you'd find those Wonders. Yep, always believed in you."

He reached into his pocket and pulled out a jaw-breaker. "On the house, boy. It'll last you all the way to St. Louis. A gift from Yount's General."

A second later, Rae Ellen Hubbell's head popped up over the side of the truck. "Will you tell them about my Wonderful in St. Louis?" she asked.

"Maybe so," I said, which seemed to please her.

Pa started the pickup and we turned onto the County Road, waving to the small crowd that had gathered at the crossroads.

Right about then, Coogie Jackson shimmied up the County Road signpost to shout his good-bye.

"Watch out for cyclones!" I heard him call.

My heart thumped hard in my chest. "I'm leaving Sassafras Springs now," I told Sal. "I'm going to St. Louis."

All of a sudden, there was Jeb running along the side of the truck. With those long legs of his, he could almost keep up. "Send me a postcard!" he yelled.

"I will!"

"I hope you go to a baseball game." He tossed something to me. "Here—catch!"

What I caught was a dried-up hedge apple. Jeb was pretty sly. He knew I couldn't look at a hedge apple without thinking of him. I tucked it in my pocket, near that folding money. Maybe there was enough to bring back a real baseball for Jeb.

"See you soon!" I told him.

The truck picked up speed, and Jeb was left in the dust, still waving.

Sassafras Springs seemed as tiny as the town on Uncle Alf's dining-room table.

"See you soon," I said aloud, even though Sal was the only one listening. I guess Columbus and Balboa told their friends the same thing when they started out on their big journeys.

"See you soon."